Corfu Capers

Sublime Retreats Romance, Volume 1

Joy Skye

Published by Joy Skye, 2019.

This is a work of fiction. Similarities to real people, places, or events are entirely coincidental.

CORFU CAPERS

First edition. December 14, 2019.

ISBN: 979-8201870706

Written by Joy Skye.

Table of Contents

REACHING OUT

From: KateDelaney@yahoo.com

To: PeterWilliams@sublimeretreats.com

Subject: Corfu Vacation

Dear Peter,

Thank you so much for reaching out. We are all looking forward to and are very excited about our upcoming trip to Corfu next month.

It will be myself, my son Scott and his girlfriend Linda, plus their two friends, Marc and Charlotte, staying at the villa. I will forward the grocery list requested shortly; I just have to double-check everybody's allergies. Please have all the beds made up as doubles.

We arrive at 10 am on the Aegean flight from Athens, and will be spending two nights there en route. Can you recommend a hotel and guide? We would like to see as much as possible whilst we are in the capital.

We will need a transfer when we land in Corfu. I don't like the idea of my son having to drive all the way to the villa when we first arrive. We need a vehicle big enough for the 5 of us plus lots of luggage; can you get a limousine there?

You see, this is going to be a very special trip; my son is going to propose to his girlfriend!

I am so excited and can't wait to plan everything. I need your help to come up with the perfect spot for this event and arrange for a photographer to be in place to snap the momentous occasion. This will happen on Thursday after we have had a few days to settle in.

Scott doesn't know this, but I have also invited 15 of our friends and relatives to come and celebrate with us. They will be staying at The Bella Mare hotel in Avlaki, which is just down the road from the villa, I believe, so will be very convenient for coordination purposes.

After the proposal, I would adore it if we could all go to a restaurant for a celebratory meal. Once I have decided on a suitable venue, I will leave it to you to make all the arrangements. Can we have some decorations, maybe some flowers, balloons, etc.? I would also love to provide our guests with rose petals to throw as the couple walk in? And, of course, we will need champagne, preferably Dom Perignon, if that's possible? If you have any other ideas on how to make this vacation beyond special, please let me know.

I look forward to hearing your ideas for my plan and, by the way, are we safe to drink the tap water on Corfu?

Best regards,

Ms Kate Delaney

From: PeterWilliams@sublimeretreats.com

To: KateDelaney@yahoo.com

Subject: Corfu Vacation

Dear Kate,

It was lovely to hear from you and I am thrilled to help you organise such an amazing event, it's going to be fabulous!

We do not have limousines on Corfu, I'm afraid, but I can offer you a luxury minibus transfer that will very comfortably accommodate your party and its luggage. The cost will be €300 each way; if this is acceptable, I shall go ahead and book?

Given the location of your villa I believe I know the perfect spot for your son to propose, there is a wonderful restaurant on the beach below called Cavo Barbaro and directly in front of it is a jetty with incredible views beyond (thinking Instagram moment here) which would be perfect. The photographer could discreetly sit at the restaurant and catch the moment from there. It is also within walking distance for your 'secret' guests to come and join the celebration afterwards.

I can arrange to have the restaurant decorated in advance and have a special table booked for you and your guests. Yes, I can provide Dom Perignon for you. How many bottles shall I order?

Please find attached a selection of trips and tours I can recommend to you to make the most of your stay on Corfu. We can also organise for one of our wonderful local chefs to come and cook at the villa one evening, maybe on the last night, so you can enjoy the amazing views from the villa terrace for your final meal.

We do not recommend drinking the tap water here. It is not dangerous, but it has a high mineral content that can upset your stomach, so I shall add bottled water to your grocery list when it comes through.

Please let me know if I can assist with anything else to make your stay as memorable as possible.

Regards

Peter

Sublime Retreats Concierge

Peter, who was sitting in his lounge as he read his emails, pulled out his diary from his bag and started scheduling the plans for Ms. Delaney's upcoming trip. The guests who were currently staying in the villa he looked after were remarkably low maintenance, and he was feeling decidedly unwanted. Every time he paid them a visit, he could barely get through the door. Mind you, judging by the photos the maid had shown him of the array of adult toys in the bedside table, it wasn't totally surprising that they didn't want his company. He didn't know what half of the devices were for, and some of them he definitely didn't want to know.

He was pretty sure they had been skinny dipping the first day he visited, hastily arranged sarongs giving the game away and not particularly disguising anything, so he now tactfully beeped his horn on arrival to give them the opportunity to cover up their sun toasted parts.

Ms Delaney, however, would appear to be much more his cup of tea. Her list of requirements would keep him busy right up until she arrived and beyond, which was how he liked it. Being essential to his guest's plans was his raison d'être.

He loved his job with Sublime Retreats; their exclusive membership and exorbitant joining fee guaranteed all his guests were noteworthy, high-end travellers, and being able to respond to their ever-increasing demands was his passion, some would even say his life. As the emails from guests came in on a daily basis leading up to their arrival, he devoured each one like it was a personal challenge, scouring them for clues and looking for opportunities to go above and beyond his fundamental concierge role.

His friends and colleagues were constantly ribbing him for his attention to detail and overkill in pre-empting his guest's needs, but, let's face it, his customer service scores and his weekly tips spoke for themselves. He knew this resulted in him being the centre of idle gossip and bitchy comments in the office and his best friend

Emma, who also worked there, was always having to defend him. It did hurt his feelings, but he tried to let it go over his head.

He and Alex, his partner, had moved to Corfu 10 years before, deciding that a more relaxed way of life was in order after being made redundant forced him to re-evaluate his priorities. They had been holidaying on the island, in the resort of Arillas on the west coast, for years and had often idly talked about their dream of moving there over a late-night glass of wine on their balcony overlooking the sea. After weeks of job searching and agonising, the pipe dream they'd always had seemed to make more sense than wasting away their lives in the London humdrum. So they made the break, selling up their flat and escaping to the sun and a more carefree way of life.

Peter had settled straight into the relaxed vibe of Corfu, despite the frustrations they came across with buying a property there. The red tape and paperwork seemed to go on forever and require a different person to stamp it at every stage. He'd made his first port of call to sign up for Greek lessons, which is where he had met Emma. He applied the same method and determination to learning this new language as he did to everything else in his life, and his language skills soon surpassed her own, despite her having been learning for several years. But they remained great friends and when the job came up at her office, she forced him to send in his CV, knowing he would be perfect for the job role. And she was right; he'd taken to it like a duck to water.

Alex, however, seemed to take no pleasure from their new surroundings, and any attempt he made at learning Greek was in the bar, where he learned to order another round quite easily. He managed to hold down a job for a while with one of the cheap end UK tour operators that had hotels there, but his newfound lethargy seeped into his work and his contract wasn't renewed for the next season.

When Alex died without warning two years ago, after 15 years together, Peter had been devastated and completely unprepared for this seeming desertion. So throwing himself into his work had been his salvation. He found that his work distracted him from the loneliness and helped him to avoid the otherwise inevitable drive back to the empty house that no longer felt like home, despite the affection from his two spoiled cats, Samson and Delilah.

Now, slowly but surely, he was opening up to the idea that there could be someone else for him, somewhere. But living on a small Greek island where opinions were around 30 years out of date made it impossible to be openly gay. It wasn't the same as London where he knew the bars and clubs where he would be welcomed.

Still, he'd been pleasantly surprised when he downloaded the Grindr app a few weeks ago, after months of indecision, to discover plenty of possibilities within the community on there. He hadn't been brave enough yet to meet up with anyone but it made him feel better that he did have options close to home. He scrolled through daily and a couple of people had caught his eye. Any day now he would click on a profile and see where it led, but not just yet.

Peter sent a quick message to the photographer he liked to use, Lucy, to tell her to pencil in the date and to give her a rough sketch of the plan so far. He knew he'd have to keep reminding her as she was a bit ditsy, but her work was fantastic and his guests were always thrilled with the results, so she was worth the extra effort involved. He was already envisaging 'the moment', as he had mentally labelled the proposal, and couldn't wait to make it happen.

He loved the diversity of the requests he received every week in his work. From sourcing and importing unique brands of bottled water, finding Greek dancers to entertain the guests in the villas, and organising wild off-road bike tours, to his ultimate request, he felt, finding a landing spot nearby for the private helicopter that brought in one set of guests. That had been a real feather in his cap when he had managed to convince the local council to let them land at the kids' football pitch on the outskirts of Kassiopi, saving his customers the hour-long drive from the airport for which they were very grateful and he was tipped handsomely.

Peter checked the time and, realising he needed to get on the road, stood up and walked over to the kitchen to open some food for his cats. Hearing the sound of a tin pop open, they both rushed in and wound themselves around his legs until he managed to empty the food into their bowls without tripping over them.

'You two love me, don't you guys? ' he said, rubbing their heads before grabbing his tablet, diary and work bag and setting out to the office, planning to stop first at the restaurant he had in mind for 'the moment' and the party afterwards. He wanted to start making the arrangements and see what extra mile he could go to, so this would be an experience to remember for all involved. He couldn't wait to tell Emma about his latest request, being stuck in the office dealing with accounts for most of the day; she loved to live vicariously through what she saw as his more glamorous role.

Kate Delany was sitting in the reading nook of her tastefully decorated English style house in Houston when she read Peter's email; he sounded as if he was the perfect concierge and, combined with her amazing planning skills, this should be a vacation to remember.

She glanced around the room, looking at the rows of romance novels she avidly read, memories floating across her mind of all the happy hours she'd spent there. Maybe she should sell up now that Scott was going to be married and living elsewhere? Although he'd moved out years ago when he first started work, he still spent a lot of time with his mum, keeping her company regularly and joining her every Sunday without fail for lunch. The house was too big for her alone and she knew that with the money she would make from selling it she could buy herself a suitable apartment in pretty much any area she liked, but as yet she hadn't made any real effort to put this idea into action.

She supposed she would see a lot less of her son after the wedding, which worried her, but the fact that her ex-husband was none too keen on their son's choice of girlfriend did make up for that a little. She couldn't wait to hear his reaction to their son's engagement to Linda Garcia. He was gonna have a duck fit and no mistake.

She had met and fallen for Danial Delaney at the Lankford Grocery Store when he was a lowly errand boy. She had been swept off her feet, captivated by his good looks and charm and, for the first time in her life, began to disobey her abusive father by sneaking out at night and meeting Danial whenever she could. After years of constant maltreatment and being made to feel that she was no better than dirt, the stolen hours with him were magical and addictive, and she couldn't wait to marry him as soon as it was legal, on her 18th birthday in the courthouse in the next town.

The intense scene that followed when they went back home to tell her family of the marriage was one she'd never forget. Her father was convulsed with a rage beyond anything she had experienced before, screaming that Danial was 'lower than a snake's belly', his face turning purple with fury, veins popping alarmingly as he hissed that Danial would never have a pot to piss in and that they could go and live in the ghetto as they deserved. When he started hurling insults at Kate, Danial had to be restrained and she'd dragged her new husband out of the house and away from her family home forever.

Her father had disowned her straight away and forbade any member of the family, including her mother, from having any contact with her, so her new husband had become her entire world. But she had been living in a bubble of love and joy and when she fell pregnant soon after, her life was complete; making a family and creating a home for the two men in her life in the tiny one-bedroom apartment they first had when they were 'too poor to paint, too proud to whitewash', as her grandmother used to say.

Danial, with his magnetism and boyish good looks, had gone on to found one of the largest real estate companies in Texas, and over the course of the years, they had moved up the property chain. When he opened his fifth office, they bought the wonderful house in Cinco Ranch, an area she had always loved and aspired to. Its leafy streets and suburban feel, along with the cachet of the community with the expensive shops and restaurants, made her feel that they had really made it and showed her Pa once and for all that she had made the right decision.

Even though her husband seemed to be working longer and longer hours and be away on frequent trips, she appreciated his reasoning that he just wanted to provide everything he could for her and their son, always bearing armfuls of presents on his return to salve any wounds left by his constant absences. She had been so very happy in her role as homemaker and mother, she hadn't given it a second thought.

When Danial had abandoned them, her world fell apart and her focus became concentrated entirely on her son; it was the only way she could cope and get through day to day, and she thanked the lord that her father was no longer alive to gloat at her misfortune as he surely would have. As time went by, the pain lessened and, after the shockingly quick divorce and the healthy settlement Danial had agreed to without demur, which included the house, she began to rebuild her life.

Scott continued to be her entire world, but as he got older and naturally spent more time away from the house, first with friends, then girls and then college, she had found she needed to fill her days and try and combat the loneliness. Even though she had been reacquainted with her family after her father's death, she didn't have any real women friends and certainly no boyfriends; she could never trust anybody enough again to let them that close. So she had joined a couple of women's groups before discovering local charities, clamouring out for women just like her. With plenty of free time and a passion for organising, she soon became in demand to organise various events and fundraisers.

She had become particularly involved with two of Houston's women's shelters, providing safety and a new start for women and their children that had been victims of abuse, and she had raised thousands of Dollars for them with various fundraisers as well as contributing as many hours as she could at the shelters.

Thinking ahead to the future, to after this holiday and a life not devoted to Scott, she realised she needed to find a new purpose in life, something that would engage even more of her time and combat the loneliness she sometimes felt. She had no idea what it might be that would assuage the feelings of remoteness from the rest of the world, but she knew she needed to be part of something else when her family life became scaled-down.

She roused herself from her reverie and walked through to the inviting country-style kitchen that she had enjoyed planning and creating so much. The room was large and airy, the wood on the high beamed ceiling complimenting the work surface she had chosen and contrasting with the pale cream cupboards. At the far end, where the large double doors opened to the conservatory, she had placed two wonderful, overstuffed sofas that made the space seem cosier, and the room had become the hub of their family life.

She turned on the Nespresso machine lined up on the counter with her many other gadgets. "I wonder if the villa has one of these," she thought to herself and made a mental note to keep a checklist of things to ask that lovely concierge before they flew out.

She was interrupted from her thoughts by her phone ringing. Dan Gillespie Sells' 'My Boy', identifying it as Scott before she dug it out from the depth of her Fendi handbag.

'Good Morning my gorgeous boy, how are you today?' she enquired with a big smile on her face as she placed her cup in the slot and pressed the button to set the coffee machine in action with its familiar buzz.

'Howdy Ma, I'm fine, thought I'd check-in. How are your plans for Corfu going? I'm getting a little nervous now, I have to admit.'

'Don't you worry about a thing, I will make sure it all runs smoothly and everything is absolutely perfect for you both. You know I won't let anything spoil it for you.'

Scott chuckled to himself 'I have no doubt regards to that Ma, none at all. It's Linda that I worry about. What if she says no? What if she doesn't like the ring? I'm as nervous as a long-tailed cat in a roomful of rocking chairs.'

'Now you listen to me, Scotty' she said as she carried her cup carefully to the table, phone wedged between her ear and shoulder 'that girl will be lucky to have you as a husband and if she's got an iota of sense, she knows that. And she will be lucky to have a Mother in Law who cares enough to plan all this for her, so she should be more than grateful. As for the ring, it cost so much she can't not love it, it's stunning.'

His eyes instantaneously flicked to the mantelpiece in his lounge, where the velvet blue box containing the ring was presently sitting. His paranoia regarding losing it had made him neurotic, and he was constantly checking it was still in there.

'OK, OK, don't get yer dander up; I just get a little jittery is all. Can you forward me all the flight details so I can let Marc and Charlotte know the timings? I'm so glad they're both coming along. It will make the whole trip a lot easier'

'It will be nice for Linda to have her best friend there to enjoy the special moment, but as for that playboy friend of yours Marc, you will have to watch him, I trust him as far as I can spit which ain't that far. You know Charlotte has always had a soft spot for him and I can handle her being all doe-eyed at the breakfast table, but not heartbroken. You can tell him from me to keep his manicured paws to himself. If he needs to let off steam, he can head into the village and charm a local peasant girl.'

Scott, sitting on his balcony overlooking Market Square Park, laughed out loud at his mother's fierceness. He knew her well enough to know she was predominantly concerned for her grand plan rather than poor Charlotte's wellbeing.

'Message received loud and clear, Ma'am; I'll give him his instructions. You never can tell, he may be swept off his feet by a luscious local beauty'

'I will believe that when I see it, that boy is a confirmed bachelor if ever I saw one. He cares far too much for his looks to have time for anyone else, as his track record to date shows. He never goes out with the same girl twice.'

'True enough. Are we still on for dinner tonight?' he said, changing the subject abruptly. 'I said I'd pick Linda up from the salon when she finishes at six and head straight over? She's looking forward to going through all the final travel plans with you.'

'Yes, that's fine; I'm making your favourite, linguine with shrimp'

'You do remember Linda is allergic to seafood, Ma?'

'Oh yes, I keep forgetting. Well, I'm sure I can rustle something else up for her. My boy deserves his favourite meal once in a while.'

Scott hung up the phone to his Mother, shaking his head as he walked back into his apartment to get some breakfast. Her organisational skills were renown throughout Houston. The fact that she insisted on organising his life wasn't something he was so keen on, but he understood. He understood that when his father left his mother for a cliché younger model all those years ago, he became the centre of her world, and her desire to be in control overtook her desire for anything else. She threw herself into organising his life as much as the charities she volunteered for on a regular basis.

He knew Linda found it tough to deal with, as had his previous girlfriends, and he was hoping that this trip would bring the women in his life closer together, or at least give them a better understanding of each other. He adored Linda and couldn't imagine a life without her in it, and was determined to make this work. When he had admitted to Kate that he was thinking to propose, she'd pounced on the idea with vengeance and had steamrollered things until now, a few short months later, he was on the brink of making the biggest commitment of his life on a beach in Corfu and he was feeling a little shell-shocked.

Tapping with practised ease at the screen of his phone, he messaged Linda to confirm the plans for the evening, tactfully suggesting she should have a big lunch in the hope that she wouldn't be too hungry when they went for dinner that night.

He finished his cereal, rinsing the bowl and placing it neatly in the dishwasher before checking the ring again and then putting it in his briefcase and heading out for his morning's property viewings. He had big hopes of shifting that imposing five-bed property in River Oaks before going on vacation so he could hit his sales target for this month and earn another bonus. His father had already messaged three times that morning to remind him of the importance of this sale, as if he needed more pressure laid on him at this point.

Working at his dad's real estate firm was something he enjoyed but, as the boss's son, he felt a real pressure to be the top salesman. He knew the other members of staff assumed he had it easy, but in reality, when he saw his father, which was periodically, Danial Delaney was a lot harder on Scott than anyone else in the firm. The burden of living up to his father's entrepreneurial talents was constant and, if he was honest, was also spurred by his need for approval from the man who abandoned them all those years ago.

Despite his growing nerves regarding proposing to Linda, he was looking forward to taking a real break, the first one he'd allowed himself since he'd started working at the firm six years before. In some ways he wished he could take a longer break, a week didn't seem long enough to truly relax, espccially under the circumstances. He really should look at taking more time out for himself, maybe Linda would appreciate it if they took a quick holiday in the fall; he'd have to ask her if she'd like that.

Linda glanced down at her phone when the screen flashed and saw it was a message from Scott. No doubt confirming darling Mummy's plans for tonight, she thought a little sharply. She gave herself a mental shake and focused on massaging the hands in front of her. As a nail artist in Houston's busiest salon, she had back-to-back appointments all day with a scant 20 minutes for lunch if she was lucky. But it paid a reasonable salary, the tips were good and, for the most part, she enjoyed her work. She liked meeting new people and hearing all about their lives. Everyone else seemed to have a life full of adventure and travel, and she longed to be like them.

She hadn't told anyone, not even her best friend Charlotte, but she'd started saving up in what she liked to call her 'possibilities pot' five years back, where she put all her tips. She now had a nest egg that she knew meant she could travel wherever she wanted and spent many happy hours online checking out destinations. She had a plan of her route mapped out, which would involve travelling for around ten months, but was unsure if she was brave enough to take that chunk of time out of her life. It seemed an impossible dream in many ways, but it was a dream that would not go away and she cherished it, keeping it close to her heart, and it fuelled the more tedious parts of her day.

If she was honest with herself, her desire to travel was the main reason she'd agreed to go on this vacation with Scott's mum. That and the fact they said she could bring Charlotte with her. It would be unbearable otherwise. She was sure having her best friend to gripe about Kate to would make all the difference. She wasn't sure if she and Scott were right for each other. He seemed so focused on his work above anything else, and she longed to be free. It didn't seem such a good match, but the fact he'd agreed to some time away had surprised her and made her feel that she should give it a little longer before making any permanent decisions about their relationship.

She understood why Kate was so hung up on her son, but he was 30 now, for God's sake, time to let go! Her constant interfering in his life could be so oppressive sometimes, and Linda had to bite her tongue regularly to avoid conflict with her boyfriend. She was looking forward to grabbing some quality time with him while they were away and had applied online to get International Driving Permits for them both so they could make use of the hire car and explore by themselves. She hoped that Kate would loosen her apron strings enough to allow this to happen, but had her doubts.

She finished up her appointment with Mrs Howser, who came in every week to see her and ran to Starbucks to grab a coffee and a sandwich. It was then that she read the message from Scott, advising a large lunch, which, reading between the lines, meant Kate had 'accidentally' forgotten about her seafood allergy yet again. She sighed to herself and finished up her lunch before running back to work. Marc was coming in this afternoon for his regular manicure and she always enjoyed seeing him.

Of all Scott's friends, he was the only one she felt she could talk to, who understood her frustrations with Kate's overbearing nature and her boyfriend's refusal to stand up to it. The boys had been friends since they were toddlers and Marc had seen the disruption caused when Scott's dad had left and the effect it had had on his mum. Even though they had chosen to go to different colleges, Scott to study Business administration and Marc to study

Veterinary medicine, their friendship had remained rock solid and they had stayed best friends.

You would think after three years of going out with Scott that she would be used to Kate by now, but it was becoming increasingly irritating. Her controlling behaviour still managed to exasperate her and make her feel helpless, as there was nothing she could seemingly do about it without causing an argument. Never mind, just a few more days to go and they'd be on their way, travelling to Europe, to Greece no less and what looked like the most idyllic island there. She couldn't wait.

As Marc Miller strode into the Fine Nails salon that afternoon, ducking his head out of habit, there was a momentary pause as every woman in the place took a second look, caught themselves doing it and then carried on with their conversations. His tall frame and broad shoulders, invariably immaculately dressed, combined with his gipsy style jet black hair and sparkling blue eyes, always caused this reaction, which he ignored. Looking across the room, he caught Linda's eye as she was finishing up with her current client.

She waved and indicated with a nod of her head that he should sit and wait for a few minutes. As he lowered himself into one of the black leather chairs in the modern monochrome seating area, the receptionist ran over as soon as she got off the phone to ask if he required any refreshment. He declined and, watching her noticeably wiggling retreat, thought "sorry my dear, you're not my type", but kept a smile on his face for when she glanced back at him, as she did every time he came in.

After a few minutes, Linda came over and he stood, looming over her, and embraced her in a big hug that had every woman in the place wishing they were her. Linda laughed to herself. She knew how attractive Marc was and the reaction of the women in the room, she wasn't blind. But she didn't see him that way now; he had become too much of a friend to her over the years for that even to be an issue. She led him over to her workstation and began the ritual of manicuring.

They chatted through the preliminary chit chat catch up as she filed his nails, Marc regaling her with tales of his patients including the young boy who'd brought his puppy in because it had found and eaten his stash of weed and the countless, nameless dates he'd had since he last dropped in.

'I don't know how you keep up,' said Linda. 'I'd never be able to remember all their names' she laughed as she pushed back errant cuticles.

A bright smile lit up his face 'I just call them all darlin', it's much easier'.

She slapped him playfully. 'Are you all set for the big trip?' she enquired. 'I'm already packed, ready and rarin' to go.'

'I'm pretty much ready; I have a few bits to pick up, some travel-sized shampoo and such before we fly. How's Ms D doing? Is she driving you nuts with all her planning yet?'

'Well, we're going to dinner with her tonight, so I'll tell you tomorrow.'

They smiled at one another in understanding. Thank God for Marc, Linda thought. He'll keep everyone in check on this trip. Except for Charlotte. Lovely sweet Charlotte who'd recently broken up with yet another boyfriend and, if Linda knew her friend at all, would be planning on a little holiday romance to get over it.

She had met Charlotte six years before when she had been dragged into the salon by her overbearing, over made-up mother, who seemed to be bullying the girl into having nail extensions which she patently did not want. The two girls had hit it off straight away and when Charlotte had snuck back a few days later, begging for Linda to remove the offending acrylics, the friendship was set in stone.

'Marc, you know I love you and trust you and would never say anything mean to you?'

'Yeess,' he said warily.

'If you go anywhere near Charlotte on this trip, I will hurt you. Badly. She's my best friend and doesn't need you screwing up her life right now.'

'Hey, hey' Marc said, putting his hands up in mock horror 'you have my word that I have no desire to do anything with Charlotte other than enjoy this vacation and watch you squirm while Ms D. plans everything to death'.

She pulled his hands back toward her so she could finish buffing his nails 'well that's ok then, as long as we understand each other,'

After his manicure, Marc decided to visit his family at their ranch in San Antonio, as he had the afternoon off from work. Pulling into the old homestead after the long drive brought back a lot of memories, not all of them good, and as he got out of the car, he steeled himself to face his father. But when he entered the kitchen through the back door, it was his mother that greeted him, looking up from the bread she was kneading and breaking into a smile. Carefully wiping a lock of hair from her eyes with her forearm, she went over to hug him, taking care not to get flour on his suit. The tiny woman all but disappeared in his embrace. How this fragile, birdlike creature had produced five strapping boys was a constant source of amazement to him.

'How ya doing, Ma?' he asked when he finally let her go 'where is everybody? It's awfully quiet around here.'

'Your Pa and brothers are up the top fixin' some fence or other. As for the women, they're off with the kids at the church picnic. I didn't much fancy going, so I stayed home to catch up on my jobs.' She smiled sweetly at him as she washed her hands, 'can I get you some tea?'

'Sure Ma, it's good to catch up with you without the mob around. I don't usually get much of a chance to talk with you. How's the old fella?' he asked as he pulled out a chair from the huge wooden table that dominated the room.

She chuckled over her shoulder at him as she filled the kettle at the sink 'He's the same miserable old sod, but that's just the way he is.'

Marc nodded silently. He had never got on with his father. Everything he had ever done had been wrong up to and including his choice to open a surgery for domestic animals. Preferring to work with cats and dogs rather than cattle was a heinous crime in his father's eyes. If his father knew the real reason why he chose to make a life for himself away from the family and the ranch it would kill him, or he would kill Marc, so it was better that he kept himself to himself although he knew his mother missed him terribly.

Which was why he was so delighted to find her alone today. At least he could spend some real quality time with her before he left for Greece.

When Scott returned to his office after what he felt was a successful viewing, the couple in question had been returning for a second look at the property and he was pretty sure he had removed any objections they may have had, he was given a stack of messages by his secretary Jean, from Danial, highlighting everything that needed to be 'put to bed' as he called it before Scott went on vacation.

He felt his blood pressure spiking as he looked through the list. The man was unbelievable; every time Scott felt he was getting somewhere with the tasks ahead, his father piled on more and more.

He had tried to bring this up with Danial before when the workload had become insane, but his father had only said 'If you want something doing, give it to someone who's busy' and walked off laughing. What made it worse for Scott was he felt there was no one he could share these concerns with. His mother became irrational if he even mentioned his father, so he tried to avoid mentioning him to her. Everyone else already thought his Pa was a bastard, but for some reason, Scott felt a loyalty to the man and couldn't bring himself to bad mouth him outside of his head.

Taking the ring box out of his briefcase and placing it on the desk as he sat down to start wading through the paperwork, he drew strength from its presence. It reminded him that very shortly he would be out of here and away from this constant, crushing stress, if only for a little while.

THE PLOT THICKENS

From: KateDelaney@yahoo.com

To: PeterWilliams@sublimeretreats.com

Subject: Corfu Vacation

Dear Peter,

Please go ahead and book the luxury minibus transfer. I assume it is air-conditioned? How will we find the driver when we arrive at Corfu airport?

Your suggestions for the proposal location sound absolutely marvellous. I've checked out the restaurant online and it all looks too good to be true. Please go ahead and book everything we have discussed.

I have confirmed the reservations for my 15 guests that are staying at the hotel. I will forward all their flight details tomorrow. Could you be a darling and book their taxis for them?

I love the look of the boat trip with Captain Yiannis; I believe he can take us along the coastline for the day? Please book that in for the Wednesday. Looking at his menu choices, I would love to request the seafood option for our group. I would also like to take up your suggestion for a chef at the villa for the last night, which sounds ideal. Please forward their menu and I will let you know what we choose for all the courses.

I have attached the grocery list of things we would like in place for our arrival. Please add 10 bottles of my favourite wine

Whispering Angel to that list and make sure they are refrigerated, along with the water.

With regards to the champagne for the celebration, I think twenty bottles should suffice, even for my family.

Can you also let me know what type of coffee machine they have there and make sure to add the appropriate pods or whatever to the list?

There are no food allergies in our group to be of concern.

Is there anything else that you believe is a must-do whilst we are in Corfu? We only have a week there and whilst I don't want to be running around for the whole trip, I certainly don't want us to miss anything either.

I gather from your emails that most of your suppliers prefer to be paid in cash. Is it safe to walk around with large amounts of money over there? I wouldn't dream of it here.

Best regards,

Kate

Ms K. Delaney

From: PeterWilliams@sublimeretreats.com

To: KateDelaney@yahoo.com

Subject: Corfu Vacation

Dear Kate,

Yes, the luxury minivans are air-conditioned. Your driver will meet you inside the arrival hall bearing a sign with your name on it. He will assist you with your luggage and take you to the transfer vehicle. I will meet you at the villa and give you an orientation of the house so that you know how everything works and can settle straight in.

I have your grocery list and will ensure everything will be in place for your arrival, but please note, we do not have 'half and half', granola or pastrami. I will substitute with local produce for you to try. I am sure you will enjoy them. The villa has a Nespresso machine, so I will order a selection of pods for you and your guests.

Everything is organised for the proposal. I have booked the restaurant that we decided on, ordered the decorations and I am meeting with Lucy, the photographer, later today just to make sure we're all on the same page.

I will be delighted to book the taxis for your hotel guests as requested. Will they be paying individually?

You have a busy week lined up with us, but I would recommend you spend some time in Corfu Town before you leave. It is absolutely beautiful and full of amazing history; I could show you around if you want to spend an afternoon there. There is also a wonderful wine tasting tour at our local vineyard that I feel you would enjoy.

I see from your notes you have hired a car with Zeus Cars to be delivered to the villa. I will call them to confirm and make sure they know where to come. Please note that if you are expecting an automatic, most of the cars here are stick shift. It might be worth double-checking with them before you arrive as automatics are in short supply. Shall I do this for you?

With regard to cash, Corfu has a very low crime rate, but I would still advise caution when out and about and using the safety deposit boxes provided in your villa. There are several ATM's in the area so we can arrange for you to take out cash as and when you need it rather than bringing it with you. It's a good idea to advise your bank that you will be travelling to avoid any problems. Another point to note that Amex cards don't always work here for some reason.

I think we have everything in place. Let me know if you feel we are missing anything.

Regards,

Peter

Peter Williams

Sublime Retreats Concierge

The night before they were due to leave, Linda received a message from Scott saying that he was working late and would have to cancel their dinner plans, again. Shaking her head, she finished packing her suitcase and gave Charlotte a call. She wanted to chat to her friend about Marc before they left anyway, so now was a good opportunity.

'Hi hun, do you fancy grabbing a bite to eat tonight? I have absolutely nothing left to eat here and Scotty is working late yet again.'

'That boy works far too hard, but I guess you shouldn't complain. Food sounds like a good idea, though. I was just going to order a pizza, and I'd only end up eating the whole thing' she laughed 'shall we do our usual?'

Linda agreed and an hour later they met at their favourite restaurant, which was within walking distance for both of them. As they walked into the gaily decorated Tex Mex, with its bright orange, colour-washed walls and the inevitable sombreros delineating every booth, they both felt a surge of excitement, knowing they didn't have to go to work tomorrow and the adventure that lay ahead, they started talking ten to the dozen, chattering over each other in a flurry of conversation.

'I can't wait for tomorrow' said Charlotte, her eyes shining with excitement as she sipped the margarita she'd ordered while deciding what to eat, looking carefully through the menu for the least fattening meals.

'I hope that excitement is due to your sense of adventure rather than your sense of getting up close and personal with Marc' stated Linda, nervously twisting her St. Christopher necklace, deciding to get straight to the point.

'I have no idea what you are talking about,' Charlotte replied, leaning forward to take a sip of her drink. 'I am in no mood to be getting it on with anyone right now. No matter what a gorgeous hunk of a man they may be, I have just split up with that idiot Jason. I only want to swim, sunbathe and relax for a while.'

Linda, who couldn't quite believe Charlotte's innocent expression, narrowed her eyes and carried on, determined to push her point home.

'I know Marc is gorgeous, but you know how he is. He's all hat an' no cattle as far as women are concerned and the last thing you need. I want you to promise me that you are not going to try anything while we are away and if I see you acting up, I'm gonna jerk a knot in your tail!'

She looked so fierce that Charlotte couldn't help but laugh 'don't you worry about little ol' me' she said, smiling at her best friend and, a decision made, putting her menu to one side 'I think you should be more concerned with the antics of Ms D ruining this trip. How was dinner with her the other night?'

'The woman is unbelievable. First, off she cooked shrimp, which I can't eat, so my "dinner"' she said sarcastically, with exaggerated air quotes 'was a grilled cheese sandwich'

'Well, at least she fed ya something,' Charlotte said, smiling at the waiter who came to take their orders. 'What about all her other plans?' she continued after he'd left.

'God knows, she was very circumspect with what she has planned beyond the flight details, apparently, we will find out when we get there. She really gets my goose with all this cloak and dagger nonsense.'

'Are you sure you're gonna manage a whole week with the woman?' Charlotte asked her friend as their Fajitas were placed in front of them.

'It's not going to be easy for sure' said Linda, rolling her eyes. 'Thank God you're gonna be there. If I look as if I'm going to kill her, drag me off and throw me in the pool to calm down,' she laughed.

They finished off their meal with delicious Churro Cheesecakes dusted liberally with cinnamon and a coffee to counteract the margaritas they'd consumed before kissing each other goodnight and going their separate ways.

It was later that night, when she was brushing her teeth before bed, that Linda suddenly realised that Charlotte had not made her that promise about Marc. 'Dang that girl,' she thought to herself as she climbed into bed. 'I hope she heeds my advice.'

Charlotte's eyes snapped open two seconds before the alarm went off. "Today's the day," she thought, feeling like it was Christmas morning. "Today is the first day of the rest of my life when I become Mrs Marc Miller.". She'd had her sights on him since the first day she'd clapped eyes on him and now she would finally have her chance. A whole week with Marc in a stunning villa in Greece; what could be more romantic? She envisioned him becoming more entranced with her as the week unfolded, the ambience of the stunning Greek island setting the mood for a full-blown romance to erupt.

This was the chance she had been waiting for, and she was going to make the most of it. She'd spent the best part of two months' salary on an entirely new wardrobe for the trip, although as a children's swim coach at the local pool she didn't earn a fortune. She was determined to knock his socks off and make him forget the never-ending trail of girls he seemed to have on his arm every time she saw him.

She had met Marc the same fateful night that Linda had met Scott. They had been on a girl's night out at Etro nightclub, dancing off her blues at splitting up with yet another hapless boyfriend, letting the 80s music lift her spirits and letting their hair down as they danced the night away. She had gone to the bar looking for Linda, who had disappeared sometime before to get some drinks and found her chatting to two good-looking men, who were leaning on the bar drinking whisky, looking very laid back and suave.

Her eyes were drawn straight away to the taller of the two, his thick black hair, the fringe falling expertly over his bright blue eyes just so, and his sensuous mouth smiling in greeting as she walked up. She'd panicked then, thinking how frightful she must look, hot and sweaty after their recent frenzied dance to Girls Just Want To Have Fun. She made her excuses and ran to the sanctuary of the bathroom, the subtle lighting doing nothing to help as she despaired at what the mirror revealed. She did her best to adjust her hair, reapplied her lip gloss and straightened out her top, which had shifted during all the jigging around.

Charlotte was insecure with regards to her looks, despite Linda's constant reassurances and the obvious effect she had on men. Her mother and elder sister had both been Prom queens, always the belles of the ball, and she had grown up feeling dowdy by comparison. Her natural tomboy leanings as a child, always happiest in jeans and preferably covered in mud, provoking their derision and merciless teasing until eventually, as a teenager, she had gradually fallen into line. Now she couldn't bear to leave the house until she looked as perfect as she could be.

That night they had both left the club alone, but whereas Linda's relationship with Scott had blossomed, Marc had put her firmly, and seemingly permanently, in the friend zone, something she had resolved to change this week.

She pushed aside the covers and bounced out of bed, stumbling sleepily towards the bathroom to shower. It was 4 am, two hours before she had to leave her apartment, but she was determined to look her best when they all met at the airport, which was gonna take some fixin'.

When they met at the United Airlines check-in desk in terminal C at George Bush Intercontinental a few hours later, Charlotte was dressed to kill. Her long blonde hair had been blow-dried to perfection, bouncing in the manner of a shampoo advert with every step she took. Her eyes were made up to maximise their wonderful shade of blue and emphasise her long lashes, her lips were glossed and her heels were roughly 3 inches too high to be practical for a long day of travelling.

Linda pulled her to one side. 'What the hell are you playing at?' she demanded. 'I thought we had agreed that Marc was out of bounds for the duration of this vacation. Those pants are so tight I can see your religion!'

Charlotte crossed her arms.'You may have agreed that but I most certainly did not,' she declared adamantly and slightly smugly, Linda thought.

'Don't be stupid' snapped Linda, rolling her eyes. 'now change out of those ridiculous shoes into something more sensible before we check in our bags. God knows when we'll see them again.'

Eventually, they were organised, Charlotte's minor concession being slightly lower heels, and they had checked in and made it through security to begin the first leg of their journey. They had a long flight ahead plus a two-hour layover at Frankfurt before they got to Athens. Linda looked over at Scott and Kate, who were standing to one side talking, and she felt unsettled.

She was sure that Kate was up to something; she was getting a strange vibe from the woman that was making her feel uncomfortable. Fair enough, she'd organised and paid for the whole trip, but the covert muttering in corners and constant glances were beginning to get to Linda, and she didn't care for it. And Scott seemed to have developed a nervous tic of some description; he kept patting the side pocket of his carry-on bag as if it was some kind of talisman.

'What's going on' she demanded of Scott when she'd pried him away to queue up at Peet's Coffee & Tea to get drinks for everyone before they boarded. 'Why are you and mummy dearest huddling in corners at every available opportunity?'

'I have no idea what you are talking about, honey. Now try to relax and let's enjoy this vacation. My Ma and me are just relishing some time together, pay us no mind. What coffee do you want?' he said absently, looking at his phone at yet another message from Danial about the River Oaks deal.

'Oh, I think I'd better have a Latte Macchiato, make it a large one,' she said, feeling wrong-footed by his casual reply.

Perhaps she was being paranoid, she thought to herself as they walked back towards the others through the miasma of perfume coming from Duty-Free, overthinking things with Scott and maybe her friend Charlotte too. She'd have to try and relax and get into holiday mode. After all, in a few minutes, she would be getting on a plane and going somewhere new, something she had been hankering for all of her life. She couldn't let Kate Delaney spoil this.

Peter was waiting in the luxurious reception of the Bella Mare hotel for the first influx of Ms Delaney's extra guests. It wasn't his job in reality, as they weren't staying at the villa, but he had nothing better to do, despite it being a Saturday night, and he felt it would make a good impression. He knew he was going beyond his job spec, but he didn't care. Little touches like this made all the difference.

He checked his phone for the time and estimated the first taxis should be there in approximately five minutes if there had been no delays. Whilst he was looking at his phone, it chimed and a notification from Grindr popped up. Someone had messaged him! He paused for a second, closing his eyes briefly before he opened the app. It was a simple 'Hi, how are you?' which was a relief, as he'd received a few that had been far too direct for his liking.

He looked through the profile of George, a local waiter at a restaurant in Kassiopi. He looked nice enough and in the right age group, but Peter still wasn't 100% sure he was ready to get out there. He touched the flame icon to send a 'tap' to let George know he was interested but would message later. He'd need time to work out what to say for a start.

Peter returned to the main screen and was delighted to note there were 18 other users within 2km of him right at that second. He smiled in amazement and glanced up just in time to see the first taxi pulling into the driveway. Standing up, pulling his shirt into place and putting on his 'meet and greet' face, he strode out and down the steps to welcome the guests.

Forty minutes later it was chaos in the reception area as fifteen exhausted and, for the most part, elderly Texans tried to understand the Greek check-in process which was no more complicated than anywhere else in the world, but seemingly took a lot of talking about.

Bill and Bobby, who apparently were Ms Delaney's cousins and obviously twins, seemed to be arguing non stop, noisily, as if they were small children bickering between themselves over anything and everything.

'Pay them no mind' said Great Aunt Eustice, a neat, prim and proper old lady wearing a large straw hat decorated with fruit, who was gazing around with a look of utter distaste and looked like she was sucking a lemon.

'They may look the same but they be two different buckets of possums.'

Shaking his head, Peter made his way to the front of the queue where Uncle Joe, an octogenarian who could benefit from the use of a hearing aid, seemed to be taking an inordinately long time.

'What seems to be the problem, Joe?' he asked and smiled at Vasso, the poor receptionist dealing with the arrival, letting her see that he sympathised with her and was there to help.

'She keeps wanting to charge me for sex,' Joe whispered, having to reach up to Peter's ear, as he was a full head taller than the old man. 'She keeps telling me it's €3 a night for the room sex, which seems mighty cheap to me. I know the country is in financial straits but even so.'

Taken aback, Peter spoke to Vasso in Greek to double-check the conversation. She answered in rapid-fire sentences and Peter began to laugh.

'Oh Joe, she's asking for the Room Tax,' he said, putting his hand on the man's shoulder. 'It's a local charge that has to be paid in cash; they can't put it on your bill.'

A big smile erupted on Joe's wrinkled face and he burst out laughing, clapped his hands together and proceeded to tell the rest of the group at top volume, adding 'I only hesitated because at my age I wasn't sure I'd get my money's worth!' and started laughing uproariously again as poor Vasso slowly went beetroot red as she realised what was being said.

Finally, they were all checked in and the bellboy was running back and forth, transporting the luggage to the various rooms, sweating under the weight. They all seemed to have packed for a month, not a week. Peter stood talking with Joe, as he seemed to be the unofficial leader of the group.

'Once you are all settled in, I have reserved a table at a taverna a few minutes' walk away for you'

'I hope it's not too far. Most of us can't walk for toffee,' laughed Joe amenably as they strolled towards the lift.

'It's 2 minutes,' said Peter, pressing the call button.

'Just turn left out of the gate and you'll see it right by the sea.'

Uncle Joe called the stragglers who hadn't gone to their rooms yet to squeeze into the small lift with him and jabbed at the button for his floor 'see you tomorrow sonny Jim!' he called as the doors closed.

Peter walked back over and gave the receptionist his card. 'Any problems or queries, give me a call; I'll pop by in the morning to make sure they aren't causing too much trouble.' Vasso gratefully took the card and thanked her lucky stars she'd be off duty before too long.

Athens airport seemed like pandemonium, the clamour and hubbub a shock after being cocooned in an aircraft for hours. But as Kate stood and watched, she began to understand that it was organised pandemonium, and very, very noisy. The rapid-fire Greek being spoken around her sounding equivalent to a non-stop argument and everybody running like their lives depended on it.

Charlotte was in floods of tears as when it hadn't appeared on the luggage belt, they had gone to the baggage handler's desk to be told her suitcase was still in Frankfurt and, of course, she was inconsolable. Kate went to join them at the desk and took charge of the situation, which was no doubt going to become a Greek tragedy before too long.

'Come on, Charlotte,' she said with a dismissive wave of her hand. 'They have all your details now and your bag will more than likely be on the next flight that comes in from there. There's nothing more we can do now, so let's get to our hotel and go out for dinner. I can't wait to start exploring.'

Charlotte looked at her, aghast. 'how can I possibly go anywhere' she moaned. 'I have nothing to wear, all my lovely clothes,' she sobbed. Kate sighed despairingly and looked at Linda, indicating with her eyes that she should step in and help.

'Come on, Lotte,' Linda said, using her friends' childhood nickname in an attempt to calm her. 'You can borrow something of mine for tonight' and, taking her gently by the arm, started walking her towards the exit. Scott and Marc had piled the bags that had arrived precariously onto a trolley and were desperately trying to steer it in a straight line after the girls.

As the doors slid open to allow them outside, a blast of humid air hit them, the heat bouncing off the pavement, and they were blinded by the rays of the sinking sun. They all stopped for an instant, transfixed by the warmth and the smell of this new country.

'Come on' barked Kate, bustling into action first and waving her clutch bag at the yellow taxis lined up a little way beyond the doors. They piled into two taxis and, after confirming the hotel address, sped downtown. Charlotte had stopped bleating at this point and was focused on fixing her make-up in her compact, so Linda was able to begin to pay attention to her surroundings. Up until now they'd been inside bland airport terminals and on planes and she hadn't had the sense of being anywhere new, but now, as the taxis zig zagged crazily through the thronging streets, she began to smile.

With the constant cacophony of horns, enormous junctions which would bamboozle the most competent of drivers and the strangely cryptic road signs, she feared for their safety in a detached yet thrilling way. Pedestrians seemed to have no hope and scurried along close to the walls of the hotchpotch of concrete buildings on narrow, badly kept pavements that would make Charlotte's heels redundant. As for the Zebra crossings, they were apparently there for decorative punctuation rather than function and people took their lives in their hands, even daring to place a tentative toe on them, causing the traffic to slow not one iota.

She knew from all her research that every big city has its invisible side with sites and areas that bear the marks of history but are hidden in the modern trappings that she could see from the taxi. Athens, with its long, turbulent history, must be such a city, she thought, and she couldn't wait to discover its unknown corners and untold stories.

Dinner that night was a relaxed affair. The receptionist of the hotel had directed them to a restaurant set in a charming small cobbled platia a few minutes' walk away that she plainly thought was the best one in the area, her enthusiastic description of the food leaving them all salivating.

They strolled happily towards the square and, as the air thickened with the smell of spiced lamb and music from a taverna nearby, they began to feel the essence of the city. The streets seemed to be coming alive on this warm summer's evening with lovers, shoppers and tourists alike and the atmosphere was quite unlike anything they had experienced before as children ran freely past them into the square.

The tables and chairs were placed around Jacaranda Trees, planted at haphazard intervals, the last of their purple blossoms dropping like confetti around them and lights were strung up between them radiating a warm glow over the scene. The table cloths were chequered blue and white to reflect the restaurant's exterior and national colours.

'My, isn't this delightful' said Kate, leading the way to a round table large enough to accommodate them and placing her bag on her chosen seat whilst she undid her matching wrap and hung it over the back of her chair.

'It certainly is,' said Linda, seating herself next to her, so distracted by the enchanting ambience of the surroundings that she didn't even consider placing herself as far away from Kate as possible as she usually would have.

The others found their places and soon the conversation was of menu choices and preferred wines, and progressed naturally to the planned tour tomorrow and finally faded as plates were brought, loaded with delicacies, halting the need for communication in preference for the enjoyment of the feast before them.

Scott looked across the table and was happy to see Linda animatedly chatting with his Mother. Her face was flushed, glowing in the candlelight, and her eyes were sparkling. She looked so happy and he didn't think that was entirely due to the amount of wine they'd consumed with dinner.

Apart from the hiccup at the hotel when it had become apparent that Kate was not going to accept them sharing a room, something that hadn't even occurred to either of them, Linda and Kate seemed to be getting on well.

'Just let her have her way for now,' he'd said when they'd managed to grab a few minutes alone together. 'This trip is so important to Kate. It's the first time she's travelled abroad since dad left and she has a certain picture in her mind of how everything will be'

'Expectation is the root of all heartache' snapped Linda, but then she softened when she saw his face fall. She was so thrilled to be travelling, surrounded by all these new sights, sounds and smells, that she couldn't give two hoots if Madam Kate wanted to be a stick in the mud.

'Don't worry,' she told Scott 'I'll behave and it will be fine. We're going to have a fantastic holiday.' He smiled gratefully and held her close for a long minute.

'Thank you,' he whispered into her hair, breathing in the familiar aroma of her favourite shampoo.

And now, with the table full of debris from the remarkable meal they'd had, their plates all wiped clean with crusty fresh bread, watching the local children running around the square as their parents chatted over coffees and ouzo's, Scott thought she was right. It was going to be fantastic. He felt his trouser pocket; yes, the reassuring feel of the box was there. He should have left it in the safe in his room, but he couldn't bear to be parted from it.

The next day was full-on. The private guided tour that Kate had arranged picked them up from the hotel at 9.30, straight after breakfast and didn't return them until a little after 6 pm. The amazing tour took in the Acropolis, the climb worth it's mesmerising views from the top and the impressive Temple of Zeus; its remaining few columns allowing you to visualise exactly how gargantuan the building had been and triumphal Hadrian's Arch between the two. They admired the impressive Parliament building on Syntagma square and watched the incredibly coordinated changing of the Evzone guards protecting the tomb of the Unknown Soldier.

After that, their guide, Eleni, led them through the crisscross of narrow streets that made up the market district. Wicker baskets of all shapes were crowded together. Hanging up high whilst below them were a perplexing collection of metal objects, from funnels to buckets, colanders and swinging trays in red, blue, green and turquoise, as well as stainless steel.

The hectic and vibrant streets were an explosion of colours and smells, crammed with produce on both sides; herb and spice emporia decorated with garlands of flamboyant dried vegetables, bright chilli peppers, looking colourful and pretty enough to be jewellery. Shops for fresh olives and feta cheese, sun-kissed fruits and vegetables, meats hanging from hooks not bearing too close inspection from the faint-hearted, basements crammed with hessian sacks of rice, beans and flours of every description.

Their guide led them down some steps, through two brown doors with no sign to indicate its presence, into what appeared to be a bunker crammed with tables, which turned out to be a restaurant that had been operating for 129 years. It was a remarkable place, with huge wine barrels taking up one wall where a flow of ruby red vino was continually being poured.

While they waited to be seated, Eleni explained to them that there were no menus as such. You were told the list of today's creations and you let the waiter know what you wanted. Everything was freshly cooked and when a particular dish ran out, that was it for the day. It was a remarkable place, and the food was fantastic, the constant flow of local customers bearing testament to its popularity over the years.

After lunch, they sat back in the luxury minivan as they set off along the Aegean coast, admiring the deep blue colours of the ocean, to explore the Temple of Poseidon. The drive along the "Athenian Riviera" to Cape Sounion and the Temple was idyllic and picturesque, a perfect end to their day.

The stream of information from the attractive young lady that was their guide was fascinating, but had become white noise by the end of the day as their brains became fried with sensory overload and tiredness.

'I'm tuckered out,' stated Marc matter-of-factly as they walked back into the hotel. 'I am thrilled that I have seen everything we've seen today, but I am ready for a shower and then a cold beer or two.'

'Well, I for one would rather a G&T,' said Kate, 'but other than that, I second your opinion. Shall we regroup on the rooftop terrace in, say, an hour?'

Their murmurs of consent were interrupted by a loud squeal from Charlotte, who had spotted her bright pink suitcase waiting patiently next to the reception desk for her.

'Oh my God, I thought I'd never see you again,' she proclaimed dramatically and threw herself upon it with such gusto it tipped over. Marc helped her and the case into an upright position and earned himself a special smile from Charlotte and disapproving looks from the other three.

That night, as they had an early start the next day, they opted to have dinner at the hotel's acclaimed rooftop terrace restaurant, affording amazing views across Athens with the Acropolis lit up in the distance.

As Kate watched the younger members of the party laughing and joking over the last of their fabulous baklava desserts, she gave a contented sigh. Sod you, Danial Delaney, she thought to herself. I was wrong; I don't need you in my life to be happy. I can't believe it's taken me all these years to realise it. She was ecstatic to be making a trip by herself; her nerves had been shot when he left her, but now she knew she could manage perfectly well and didn't need a man in her life for anything and she was enjoying this newfound feeling of independence.

From: KateDelaney@yahoo.com

To: PeterWilliams@sublimeretreats.com

Subject: Corfu Vacation

Dear Peter,

Many thanks for your recommendations for hotel and guides here in Athens. We have had a wonderful time and are hugely excited to continue our journey to Corfu tomorrow morning.

The tour of the local vineyard sounds lovely. Can you please book in all of us, including my hotel guests, for Saturday? I shall leave you to organise the necessary transport.

Please find attached our menu choices for the last evening.

Are there any bugs or critters in Corfu we should be wary of?

I look forward to meeting you tomorrow.

Regards,

Kate

From: PeterWilliams@sublimeretreats.com

To: KateDelaney@yahoo.com

Subject: Corfu Vacation

Dear Kate,

I am thrilled to hear you are enjoying your trip so far and eagerly await your arrival with us tomorrow. Everything is confirmed and going to plan.

I met your guests when they arrived at the hotel. Please be assured they are all well and happy.

I have booked the vineyard tour for Saturday as requested; the minibus will collect you first from the villa at 10 am and then go down to pick up your hotel guests before taking you to the Ropa Valley.

We do have the usual mosquitoes and the odd snake, but nothing that a blast of Deet and keeping the screen doors shut doesn't combat.

Best regards,

Peter

Sublime Retreats Concierge

MONDAY

The next day dawned bright and blue, promising another Mediterranean day of warmth and sunshine. After the full buffet breakfast, the group had arranged to meet up in the reception area to wait for their taxis to the airport. Scott arrived in good time, leaving Marc in their shared room arranging his hair, a constant source of amusement to him; his friend took longer to get ready than Charlotte, who was renowned for spending hours perfecting her look.

He had had to run back to the room to collect the ring which he'd slept with, keeping it safe under his pillow, and had a minor panic attack until he found it wedged down the back of the bed. He pulled it out with a sigh of relief, causing Marc to throw a concerned look in his direction, but he chose to say nothing and continued to brush his hair into submission.

As Scott walked into the reception, he saw Linda sitting by one of the picture windows reading a book and he paused, admiring her beauty and the way the sun was catching the different highlights in her long auburn hair. 'I am such a lucky guy,' he thought to himself and, smiling, he walked over to where she was sitting.

'Good Morning beautiful. Are you ready for the next stage of our adventure?' he queried, bending down to kiss her cheek.

'I certainly am,' she said, waving a Greek Islands guidebook at him. 'I'm getting the lay of the land from here so we know where to go exploring.'

'I wouldn't worry too much about that; I'm pretty sure Ma has it all in hand.'

She looked hard at him, frowning. 'We are going to get some time to ourselves, aren't we, Scott? I thought the whole point of getting those International Driving Permits was so we could go off exploring by ourselves. I've been reading about this amazing abandoned village high up in the mountains that I'd love us to go and see. It looks incredible.'

Scott shifted and looked uncomfortable; he hated being caught between his Ma and Linda. 'I am sure there will be some free time for us, sweetheart,' he said, hoping to placate her. 'Oh look, there's Charlotte and mum. Over here!' he shouted to get their attention and was saved from any further difficult discussions by his phone ringing. Seeing that it was his Pa he walked outside to get a little privacy. He had promised Linda he wouldn't be working on this trip, but he couldn't see how he could avoid it at this crucial point in such a big deal.

'Hey Pa, what are you doing up at this time?'

'I'm concerned about the River Oaks deal. It's taking too long,' he said without preamble. 'I think you should go check with their attorneys tomorrow first thing.' Scott started pacing up and down the pavement in front of the hotel. The noise from the passing traffic made it difficult to hear properly, and he had to strain to understand what his father was saying.

'Pa, first off, I left everything in place. I have left a list of things to follow up on Jean's desk. Secondly, I am in Greece. I am on vacation, remember?'

There was a sharp intake of breath and what might have been a curse, but it was hard to tell over the echoes on the line.

'God damn it, Scott, I don't approve of this timing. This deal is far more important than you and your mother gadding around Europe on a whim.' He could almost picture his father's face screwed up in agitation, leaning back in his throne style leather chair in his office.

Scott stopped pacing and took a deep breath, debating the wisdom of whether or not to tell his father the real reason for the trip. Up until now, he had opted not to say anything. He was aware his father thought he could do a lot better than Linda. He'd made that quite clear after the one meeting they had had two years ago when he had deigned to meet them for dinner. The stilted conversation over the meal and the dismissive tone he'd used about the girl afterwards left Scott in no doubt of how his father felt.

'Well, I'm here now. I will email Jean and make sure everything is proceeding as it should. I suggest you get some sleep and quit worrying over my work. If there are any problems, Jean will let me know faster than green grass through a goose.'

Danial harrumphed. 'Well, I guess that'll have to do. Keep me posted.' And with that he hung up, leaving Scott feeling like a four-year-old that had just been told off, a common reaction to interactions with his father. He could never be good enough in his father's eyes. He stood for a while, gazing into the middle distance, trying to rediscover the equilibrium of moments before and wishing for the millionth time that he could escape from the pressures of work. The urge to run away and abandon it all crept up on him yet again until the blaring of a horn from a bus trying to squeeze between badly parked cars on the street brought him back to the present and he made his way back inside.

Linda, who was watching Scott pacing through the window, was pretty sure he wouldn't want to upset his mum by taking time out for them this trip, but more and more she was finding that she didn't care. In fact, if that was the case, she'd be more than happy to head out on her own and to hell with them! But now wasn't the time for that particular conversation. They had a plane to catch and an island to get to; the state of their relationship could wait until they got back home.

Charlotte and Marc were the last to join the group and as they walked in arm in arm, pulling their luggage behind them. Linda couldn't help but think they did make a cute couple. Despite the height difference, they were both so attractive they seemed right somehow. "Maybe I should let Charlotte throw herself at him?", she thought to herself as they walked out to their taxis, "it's probably time he settled down and God knows Charlotte could do worse; he's such a nice guy when you get to know him".

'Ms Delaney,' the receptionist called, 'your taxis are here.'

'Thank you,' she replied. 'Come on y'all, let's get going!'

Scott and Kate jumped into the first taxi, leaving Linda behind to get in the second car with the other two. She realised she should be miffed, but pushed that thought to the back of her mind. Charlotte and Marc were in the back giggling together like a couple of school children, but she was too distracted to pay them much mind as she tried to focus her thoughts on making the most of this trip. It was the first time she'd left the States, and she was determined to enjoy every single moment of it, whatever anyone else did.

In the taxi ahead, Kate took advantage of their time together and said to Scott 'right, everything is in place, you'll go for a walk along the beach with Linda on Thursday, walk her out on the jetty there, drop to your knees and do the deed. The photographer will capture the moment and we'll all be waiting for you to come and announce your nuptials in the restaurant.'

Absently patting his bag pocket where the ring was currently ensconced, Scott grinned, but looked worried. 'It sounds simple enough Ma, I really hope she appreciates it, that's all.'

'It will be fine,' Kate responded with a close-lipped smile. 'I have everything in hand, don't you worry. Nothing can go wrong.'

It seemed to Linda later that morning as the plane circled and started its descent to what looked to be a very short runway, that the flight had taken less time than the taxi ride to the airport. The battle through the Athens rush hour had seemed interminable, yet the flight was over before the stewardesses, all immaculate in their navy blue dresses with scarves neatly cinched around their necks, had barely had time to serve the coffee.

As the fasten your seatbelt light pinged on and the small plane sank lower and lower, she took in the ridiculously azure waters of the Ionian Sea and marvelled at the remarkable greenness of the island below her. It was breath-taking beyond expectation. She smiled to herself and, all the worries she had about her and Scott's relationship fading into the background, she gathered together her belongings eagerly, ready to disembark.

When they reached the exit, once again they were hit by a wall of heat and incredible light, causing everyone to fumble blindly for sunglasses as they walked down the steps of the plane to the bus, waiting to take them to the terminal. It made her laugh as the building was only a few feet away and yet they still were made to cram onto the buses like sardines with all the other passengers, to be ejected a few seconds later and herded up the slope into the tiny building with a gaggle of locals and a few backpacking types to see the baggage reclaim belt immediately in front of them.

Corfu airport seemed tiny compared to the gigantic building with its never-ending tunnels and security checks that they'd met at so many hours before.

As promised, there was a smiling driver wearing smart blue shorts and a white polo shirt and holding up a printed sign displaying **Ms Delaney and Party – Sublime Retreats** waiting for them as they exited the baggage reclaim. To everyone's relief, all the suitcases had arrived in one piece.

The driver shook them all by the hand and introduced himself as Spiros and then proceeded to skillfully lead them through the chaos; so many nationalities, so many families and groups of friends, all looking worried as they searched for their coach transfers or loved ones, and led them to the cool of their private minibus and whisked them out of the airport in no time. They all were grateful for the cold bottles of water thoughtfully provided for them, much needed in this sudden shocking heat, as they settled with relief into the comfortable seats.

The drive through town was a little hectic, but they were distracted by the remarkable views that met their eyes when they pulled out onto the road that led along the seafront. The view of the Old Fortress, standing proudly, if a little corroded, out on a promontory and framed by the distant mountains took their breath away.

Spiros was a mine of information as they inched along in the slow-moving traffic; he seemed inordinately proud of his home and kept up a running commentary of each landmark that they passed. The Old Fortress had housed the original town and dated back to Byzantine times, he told them, and, nodding in its direction as they rounded the bend, 'This is the Palace of St Michael and St George. It is from when the British were in charge here and is built with Maltese limestone.' They admired the grand-looking building as the traffic freed up a little and they passed through an archway and along the port road where several gargantuan cruise ships were moored up, ejecting bewildered tourists by the hundred.

As they left the city behind and started to drive up the winding coastal road, the view became more impressive with each hair rising turn. Swathes of olive groves dominated on the left with the stunning coastline running in parallel on the right, the occasional small village perched precariously along the route making every bend a revelation. They were all dazzled by the lushness of the island and the intense blue of the languid seas dotted with sailboats gently making their way to their various destinations, made to look insubstantial by the larger ferries further out, steaming along with a purpose.

They were beginning to fidget and stretch out their legs when, an hour later, they turned off the main road and the minibus made its way along a rough, dusty, unpaved track until it arrived at some impressive ivory iron gates, which swung open after sticking for a split second, at the beep of the horn, and admitted them into the peaceful, walled gardens that led to their villa, their little slice of heaven for the next week.

With cream walls and pale, green shutters, the wide building was roofed with terracotta tiles and was the perfect picture of a Greek house, the gardens full of lavender and other scented bushes they couldn't quite recognise, carefully planted around sculpted olive trees. The prominent portico was supported by wide columns and there, in the shade, was Peter, waiting to greet them.

He always got a little nervous at this point because you could never know what sort of people would be getting out of the minibus, and it was his responsibility to make this group happy for the next week, whatever it took. He knew from experience that no matter how many emails flew back and forth in the weeks leading up to the holiday, you couldn't gauge a person's character until you met them in the flesh.

He had been at the villa preparing for their arrival all morning, walking around and checking every aspect to make sure it was perfect. Conscientiously flicking on every lamp to make sure they worked, turning on every electrical item and making sure the Wi-Fi was running at a good speed, placing fresh Sublime Retreats notepads and pens on every bedside table. He worked his way through his extensive checklist until he was satisfied that everything was shipshape and, as his last job, he double-checked the delivery from the grocery store to make sure nothing had been missed off the list and put all the wine in the drinks fridge before setting out a welcoming meze for his guests.

Now he walked forward to meet them, licking his lips and smiling, ready to make a good first impression. The first to leap out was a tall, nice-looking man with short brown hair and kind brown eyes whose immediate reaction was to smile warmly at Peter and walk over to shake his hand.

'Hi, I'm Scott, Kate's son; it's wonderful to meet you. I gather you've been an absolute rock helping my mother organise this extravaganza?'

Peter blushed. 'It has been an absolute pleasure, really not a problem. I'm sorry about the gates, there seems to be a slight fault but not to worry, I can get them checked out in no time.'

And they turned to look at the others, who were emerging one by one from the minivan, stretching and shaking numb limbs to life. A tall, slender, older woman with a chic bob of natural-looking auburn hair and appearing un-creased and made up despite the long journey was taking control of the unpacking process, much to the driver's agitation. This had to be Kate; he thought to himself and strode across to make himself known.

'Hi Ms Delaney, I'm Peter. It's an absolute pleasure to meet you!' he exclaimed a little too over the top, even to his ears. Ms Delaney turned, and with a disarming smile, gracefully took his proffered hand

'Call me Kate, please,' she said. 'I am so happy to finally be here.' She turned to the rest of the group who had disembarked and said, 'everybody this is the lovely Peter who has been an absolute angel helping me plan this vacation. Peter, this is Linda, my son's girlfriend and her friend Charlotte who has come along for the ride.'

There was a flurry of handshaking and how do you do's and then Peter turned to the last member of the group and stopped dead in his tracks. Standing to one side, a little away from the group, stretching out the last of the journey's stiffness, was the most stunning man he'd ever clapped his eyes on.

'Marc, Marc' Kate called, 'come over and say hello to our wonderful concierge Peter'. Marc turned and loped over to join them, smiling broadly, his shock of wavy, wild black hair bouncing with each stride.

'Pleasure,' he said, shaking Peter's hand, his blue eyes twinkling with mischief.

'He's the one most likely to cause trouble,' said Kate. 'You'd better warn the locals to lock up their daughters', to which Charlotte exploded into a fit of girlish giggles. Peter bit down his desire to focus on Marc and put his professional head on, determined not to screw this up by drooling over the attractive man smiling at him.

'Come on everyone, let's get you inside' he said as he grabbed the handles of two of the nearest suitcases, turned and strode towards the villa.

At that moment, a large tabby cat came running out from the bushes and began to wrap itself around their legs, demanding attention in true feline fashion.

'What is *that* doing here?' Kate demanded, wrinkling her nose; whilst Marc bent down to scratch the purring animal's head.

'Oh, that's Sarah,' explained Peter. 'She's the villa cat, and she's no bother.'

'Well, she can't stay here. My Scotty is highly allergic, and I do not want him going into anaphylactic shock. You will have to have her removed!'

Pete was nonplussed; his brain was racing trying to think how and where he could transport the poor mite. She'd never been a problem before. His two spoilt beasts would freak and not welcome an intruder in their home, and he had no idea where else to place her for the week. This was not an auspicious start.

'Now Ma, I haven't had a reaction to an animal since I was roughly three, don't you think you're overreacting a little bit?' Scott said, walking forwards and putting his arms around her.

'I only want everything to be perfect,' she wailed into his chest. 'We can't have anything throwing the plans out'. This caused Linda to roll her eyes at Charlotte, who smirked and turned her face away.

'Don't worry Ms D,' said Marc, standing up, 'if she's any bother I will deal with her. Scott doesn't have to touch her. I'm sure it'll be fine.'

Looking unconvinced but not wanting to give further cause for the collection of puzzled and concerned looks she was getting from everybody else, she turned to Peter. 'OK young man, lead the way,' she said and, after a slight hesitation, he continued through the ornate green front door.

Feeling relieved that this apparent disaster had been diverted and feeling even more attracted to the dashing Marc, seeing him as Sarah's saviour, he steeled himself for the grand tour.

This was the part Peter loved, what they called the wow factor. As you entered the front door of the villa into the living area, you were greeted by the sight of the huge picture windows, which formed a frame for the stunning views out to sea and the mountains of Albania beyond. The five of them were suitably impressed, standing stunned gazing at the view, so he allowed them time to soak it all in before adeptly moving them on to the orientation tour of the rest of the magnificent villa.

'Through here we have the master bedroom,' he said, walking through the doorway off the lounge and into a large airy room decorated in shades of forest green. 'It has an en suite bathroom and dressing room and here,' he said, opening the French doors, 'is a private terrace.'

'I love this space,' said Kate, feeling immediately at home in this calm oasis. 'I shall have this room. You kids can choose between the others, which I believe are downstairs?' she asked of Peter.

'Yes they are, follow me and I will show you the rest of the house.' And he led them back through the lounge and down the open plan staircase.

'All the rooms have individual colour schemes, their own bathrooms and a seating area through the patio doors,' Peter said as he led them into the first bedroom, which was decorated in delicate shades of blue. 'The owners have worked very hard to make sure each room is special and I think they have done an amazing job,' he added as they proceeded to view the other three bedrooms along the corridor.

'What's through that door there?' asked Kate, pointing to the one closed door along the hallway.

'That's the laundry room,' he said, opening the door so they could peek inside. 'All the instructions for the appliances are in that drawer there, but if you don't want to deal with your washing, your maid will happily do it for you.' He continued along the hall.

'Here we have the gym and next to that is a fully equipped office should any of you need it.'

'That's perfect, I will no doubt have to do some work this week' Scott said, looking apologetically at Linda, who shrugged nonchalantly and carried on walking after Marc, who had reached the room at the end of the corridor.

'Come look at this y'all' he called excitedly, and they all hurried to join him in the huge media room. With the largest flat-screen TV they had ever seen and an enormous, comfortable looking corner sofa, it was quite impressive. 'Look, there's a PlayStation! Scotty boy, we are definitely having a game night this week!'

'Well, I have to say I'm blown away,' said Kate, smiling at Peter. 'I knew the house would be a certain standard, but this place has exceeded my expectations on every level.'

Peter glowed under the praise for the villa as if it was his own creation. 'Well, there's still more to see,' he said, 'follow me', and he walked back towards the stairs.

'Linda, you and Charlotte can take the first two rooms and the boys can argue over the other two,' said Kate, sweeping back up the stairs after Peter.

Linda paused, pulling Scott to a halt with her hand. 'Is she for real, expecting us to sleep in different rooms for the entire week?' she demanded. 'I've never heard anything so prehistoric!'

Scott was unsure how to respond, as it was altogether obvious by her comment that this was Kate's plan, yet he didn't know how to justify his mother's bizarre thinking.

'Sweetheart, my Ma is a little old-fashioned to be sure, but what can we do? This is her vacation, let's face it, she's paid for everything and when all is said and done I don't want to upset her right now and spoil the trip for her.'

'No, you never want to upset her, do you, Scott?' she snapped. 'Maybe you should start worrying about upsetting me once in a while', and with that, she stormed upstairs after Kate.

'That's your rock and your hard place right there, buddy,' said Marc, smiling at his friend's downturned face. 'You are never going to win that argument.'

Scott grimaced 'never a truer word spoken, mate. I really don't know how to make Linda understand. You remember how Ma was when dad left? It took years for her to pull herself together and pouring all her focus and attention on me was how she coped and got through it. I know Linda thinks I should stand up to her, but it would be kicking her in the teeth. I just can't do it.'

Marc shook his head 'I think you only need to sit down and explain that to Linda, she's an amazing girl and I believe she'll be there for you, and, after all, if you are going to pop the question this week, you need her on your side.'

At that point, Charlotte, who'd scampered off after Linda, reappeared on the stairs, bikini already on. 'Come and see the pool guys, it's amazing, last one in is a pussy!' she yelled and ran back up the stairs. The two boys smiled at each other and walked up to join the girls.

They found Kate and Linda chatting with their concierge in the sizable kitchen area. They were standing around the granite-topped central island, drinking champagne and nibbling on an appetising Greek meze spread across its surface, so the boys both took a plate and joined them.

'We are so close to Albania at this point you have to be careful as your cell phones will flip over to Albanian time and, as they are an hour behind us, it can be a bit confusing,' Peter was just saying. The patio doors behind the girls were open, leading to a terrace with steps down to the pool area from where delighted squeaks and splashes were echoing back up to them.

'Sounds as if Charlotte is having fun already,' Marc said. 'I think we should all get ready and join her. A swim will wash away this travel fatigue.'

'Your car is being delivered at 6 pm' said Peter. 'I've made sure it's a five-seater as requested and double-checked it's an automatic for you. I've also left a copy of your itinerary for the week right here', he pointed at the dining table. 'And Scott, I believe you are the driver of the group, so can I show you how our pre-programmed GPS works? It has all your destinations on it already so you should have no problems getting around.'

Peter finished showing Scott the simple to use GPS and got ready to leave. 'I will pop back in the morning, about 10 o'clock?' he inquired, looking at Kate.

'Yes, I'm sure some of us will be up by then,' she laughed, 'although I'm not sure which zone my body clock is in right now.'

'That's fine. If you need me earlier, please feel free to call. We can go through your plans for the week and after you've all had breakfast, I can take you on a tour of the local area so you can get your bearings' he said, picking up his clipboard and bag and heading towards the door. 'Have a great first day and if you need anything at all, please don't hesitate to call. I'm available 24/7,' and with that, he left them to settle in.

Within no time at all, the group were lounged around the pool on the smart wooden sunbeds, soaking up the warmth from the afternoon sun and enjoying the sound of the invisible cicadas proclaiming the afternoon heat.

'Did you all remember to make your playlists?' asked Kate from her sunbed. 'I've made a rota. Marc, you can play yours today. I'll send you all the list so you know whose turn it is.'

As Marc obediently connected his phone to the villa's Sonos system and the strains of Brittany Spears came through the hidden speakers, Linda leant over to Charlotte. 'I can't believe she's made a rota,' she hissed.

Charlotte smiled at her friend. 'Well, it makes some kinda sense I guess, we all have very different tastes, and it's better than listening to her classical nonsense all week!' 'This is the life' she added with relish, leaning back onto the sunbed, looking in her compact and smoothing more sunscreen carefully onto her face.

'It certainly is,' Kate agreed. 'Linda, put on more sunscreen please; we don't want you looking burnt in all the photos,' she said, looking meaningfully at Scott. He immediately moved to help Linda put more cream on her back, but she shooed him away with a flap of her hand.

'I think I know whether I need to put on more cream or not. I'm not a child!' she retorted. As she said it, she realised that she sounded so petulant she was acting childlike, but she didn't care.

She was sick to death of Kate's constant interference and her boyfriend's inability to do anything without his mother's say so.

'What's the plan for tonight?' Marc asked in an attempt to defuse the atmosphere that was building up around them and used his phone to skip to 'Walking on Sunshine' to try and help lighten the mood.

'Oh, tonight we are going to a wonderful restaurant called "To Psari" said Kate, carefully trying to pronounce the alien words. 'It's supposed to be the best seafood restaurant on the island, I can't wait to try their Calamari!' she exclaimed, not registering the look of horror on Scott's face and the drop in temperature as Linda threw her an icy glare. 'In fact, I think I shall go and unpack and have a shower and get myself organised for this evening. We're leaving at seven so make sure ya'll are ready in time' she said, standing up and, wineglass in hand, walked back up to the villa.

'She is unbelievable,' exploded Linda after Kate disappeared. 'She knows bloody well that I am severely allergic to seafood, yet she makes that our first stop! She's trying to kill me, I swear.'

'Now, now,' Scott said, standing up and trying to calm her. 'She's forgotten, that's all, it's nothing personal.'

'If you believe that, then you are more of a damn fool than I think you are!' Linda shouted and with that, she stormed off in search of solitude, away from her stupid boyfriend and his domineering mother.

Charlotte found her a few minutes later, sitting on the secluded terrace outside her beautiful blue bedroom that exuded peace and tranquillity; she hoped her friend was soaking some of the atmosphere up.

'Are you OK' she asked, waving the bottle of white wine and the two glasses she'd grabbed on her way through the kitchen. 'I thought you could use some of this,' she said, plonking them down on the table and slopping large servings into each glass.

'Look, I know she could make a preacher cuss, but she is Scott's mum. I think you need to find a way of accepting her the way she is if you two are going to spend your life together.'

Linda gratefully took a large gulp of wine from her glass and looked at her friend, her eyebrows arching in concentration 'You're right, you know. Not about accepting her, about the fact that I can't. And what that means for me and Scott.' She took another swig. 'You may have hit the nail on the head there. I'm not sure if Scott and I are right together and I think this trip is proving that to me once and for all.'

Charlotte stared at her friend, eyes widened in shock; she couldn't believe what she was hearing. Linda and Scott had always seemed rock solid, a couple she looked up to and hoped one day to emulate.

'Steady on Linda, we're all tired, jet-lagged in fact, so maybe you should take a step back, wait for a little and see how this week goes. Take this opportunity to get to know Kate a bit better?'

Linda sat there in silence, fiddling with her necklace and staring out into the distance for a while.'You are absolutely right, Charlotte, but the thing is, I'm not sure if I want to.'

A few minutes after 6 pm, the buzzer sounded and, looking into the console's video screen, Scott saw it was the Zeus car hire people with their car. He pressed the button to open the gate, but nothing happened. He pressed it again more firmly, and it began opening, shuddering every inch of the way. He went out to meet them and couldn't help but laugh when he saw the car parked in the driveway.

'My God, that's tiny.' he said to the woman who was filling out the contract. She looked at him in surprise, her mouth forming a small O underneath her prominent nose.

'But it's a group D, it is what you ordered, it's one of our biggest cars, Sir.'

'I'm sorry. I didn't mean to sound rude. It's what we would call a compact,' said Scott. 'It's fine, where do I sign?'

Paperwork completed, he went back into the villa and called out to the others. 'Come on ya'll, the car's here. Let's get ready to go to dinner.'

Scott was very grateful that they drove on the same side of the road as he steered the car carefully out through the gates and up the winding track, through the olive groves to what was laughingly called the main road. He'd seen footpaths wider back home. The restaurant they were going to was only a 10-minute drive away according to the insistent, female voice on the GPS, and he was happy it was a short trip for their first run out. It gave him a chance to get used to the car and, quite frankly, the atmosphere inside it wasn't great.

Linda hadn't spoken to him much all afternoon and was squashed up on the back seat with Charlotte, who seemed intent on flirting with Marc, who, although wasn't encouraging her, certainly wasn't stopping her either. His mother, as usual, was oblivious to the charged atmosphere and was sitting next to him, chattering away and giving a delighted running commentary on everything that they passed.

The restaurant, when they found it, was charming; perched on the edge of the water in a beautiful little bay that was glowing in the orange light from the setting sun. The small white building with blue shutters had a terrace, edged with large pots of herbs that extended out into the water, and they followed the pebble bordered path in that direction to find their table. Kate took her place at the head of the table when the waiter showed them to their seats and Charlotte took the opportunity to grab the chair next to Marc, leaving Linda scowling as it meant she had to sit next to Scott. They took their time perusing the menu, opting to try a variety of starters at the waiter's suggestion. Linda was still sulking at the choice of the restaurant but, to be fair, she'd managed to find several dishes she wanted to try.

'That feta in filo pastry with honey sounds amazing!' she said to the table in an effort to kick start the conversation and make the evening more tolerable. She was very aware that she wasn't making things easy for Scott, but she knew it was equally hard on their friends as well, and she didn't want to ruin it for them. The situation wasn't their fault.

And as is the way, with good food and wine in an exotic setting, with the provocative perfume of basil and oregano filling the air around them, they all began to relax and start to enjoy themselves. Linda eventually even managed to respond with a smile to Scott's tentative looks and had to laugh at Charlotte's flirtatious and outrageous storytelling about the kids she taught at the pool in her attempts to charm Marc.

'This kid was desperate to beat the others and kept turning early and I said to him after 'You missed the wall. Why didn't you go back to touch? And he said, "The wall was too far away, and I wanted to beat the others". I had to laugh. He's only eight, but I think he's gonna go far! And there was this other kid, a little girl who's recently started with me, and last week she was doing the butterfly all the way through our breaststroke session and I said to her "Why are you doing a different stroke than everybody else in the pool?" And bless her heart, she said "I thought they were doing it wrong!"'.

As the evening began to wind down, Kate raised her glass in a toast. 'Here's to a fantastic vacation. I hope ya'll enjoy what I've organised for you and that this week is one we shall never forget!'

Linda clenched her teeth and clinked glasses with everyone whilst thinking that she was going to take every opportunity to get out by herself and explore this beautiful island. For her sanity, if nothing else, she could not - would not - spend the entire week being dictated to by Kate Delaney. She would speak to Peter the concierge in the morning and see what he could suggest for her. She'd take the local bus if she had to.

Peter was back at home but still working on his laptop, answering queries from upcoming guests and checking everything was in order for the grand proposal on Thursday. He'd ensured that the flower arrangements, petals and balloons would be delivered to the restaurant in the morning so he would have plenty of time to go and do the decorating before the event.

His mind was distracted, though; his thoughts kept flicking back to the cobalt blue eyes and the cheeky grin of Marc, no matter how hard he tried to push them back in the right direction. He'd even stalked him on Facebook, scrolling through all his photographs and looking for clues about his personality. How sad was that? 'Pull yourself together, man,' he muttered to himself as his phone rang.

'Good evening, Sublime Retreats, Peter speaking' he responded on automatic pilot.

'Hi Petey, it's Lucy. I'm calling from my sister's phone coz I have no idea where mine is right now.'

Peter sighed. He hated being called Petey, and he hated disorganisation even more. 'Hi Lucy, are you all set for Thursday? I'll be at the restaurant an hour before "the moment" putting up decorations so I can meet you there.'

'Slight problem, Petey. My car's given up the ghost. But don't panic, I've checked and there's a bus I can catch that will get me there in time.'

Groaning inwardly but trying to remain calm, Peter said, 'are you sure it will get you there on time? You know how unreliable these services can be.'

'Chill out, Petey, it will be fine. I use the buses a lot, my car spends more time in the garage than on the road, I will be there!'

'Ok, I guess that will have to do. Any problems and I mean any at all, please call me. If need be, I'll send a taxi to get you. I don't have time to drive to town but I can't have this go wrong!'

Putting his phone on to charge with an exasperated sigh, he tried not to worry too much about Thursday. Lucy was out of his control, but everything else was arranged. He'd popped into the hotel after leaving the villa today and found the other group having a wild old time around the pool and emptying the pool bar of its contents. Except for Great Aunt Eustace, who was sat in the shade of an umbrella surveying the debauchery, looking disgruntled. Uncle Joe seemed the most inebriated, but was surprisingly coherent, and Peter was fairly sure he'd taken on board the instructions to keep a low profile, but he had left a note at reception to be on the safe side. He didn't want that lot staggering down the beach at the wrong point and spoiling it all, so he had organised some excursions to keep them out of the way for the next couple of days.

A trip to the golf course for the men had been set for tomorrow. Corfu had a reputedly good course, and they were all clamouring to go, although Peter was finding it hard to imagine this boisterous group being welcome in the sedate atmosphere of the golf club and he hoped there would be no repercussions from the booking.

The women in the group had preferred the idea of going into Corfu town for a spot of retail therapy; he'd assured Eustace that they could also visit some churches to make her more enthusiastic about the trip. He had arranged for one of his local guides to meet them in front of the inevitable McDonalds and show them around the old streets where the best jewellers, boutiques and craft shops were hidden, so that should keep them happy for the day.

For the Wednesday he had arranged for them all to go out on a boat trip from Kassiopi to a local sandy beach called Kalamaki, where he knew they would be plied with copious amounts of alcohol and kept entertained with silly drinking games, most of which involved staggering up and down the beach after downing shots of dubious content, so that should be enough to keep them occupied until the big day. Poor old Eustace would have to take her chances with that one, but hopefully, she would derive enough entertainment from reprimanding the others and feeling righteous in her sobriety.

TUESDAY

The next morning, Scott was up before dawn. He hadn't slept well. A combination of jet lag and nerves about the proposal, plus the fact he knew how upset Linda was, had kept him tossing and turning all night until, seeing it was getting light, he gave up and went upstairs.

He made himself a coffee and, taking his cup and a book, went and sat on the terrace. But he couldn't concentrate on reading and ended up mesmerised, watching the amazing colours of the sunrise and the remarkable beauty of the distant Albanian mountains, the vision of which seemed to be transforming with the changing light. 'This is such a perfect spot' he thought to himself. 'We are so lucky to be here.'

He knew his mother had done reams of research into the various locations available this summer through Sublime Retreats and, even though Corfu hadn't been the cheapest option for them as the villa was huge and the flights weren't cheap, she had been adamant that this was the place where he should ask Linda to marry him.

Standing by the railings, he could just make out the beach below through the trees. The beach where, in two days, he would drop down on one knee and ask Linda to spend the rest of her life with him. It was quite frankly terrifying, and he was breaking out into a cold sweat just thinking about it. He decided he should go for a run to clear his head and calm his nerves and, not wanting to disturb anybody, crept as quietly as possible back downstairs to change into his running gear.

On his way out through the gates, a vivid green Vespa pulled to a halt next to him and a young man, dressed in dark blue shorts and a vest, greeted him with a hearty 'Kalimera' and a broad smile.

'I am Thomas, the gardener and pool boy,' he said in remarkably good English. 'I go now to clean the pool. I will be quiet so I no wake up the family,' he grinned at Scott.

'That's fine, bud. I'm going off for a run, but everyone else is still in bed.' Scott, realising he was over annunciating and doing a ridiculous mime whilst he said this, in his embarrassment gave an abrupt wave to Thomas, stuffed his earbuds in and jogged off down the track in search of clarity and inner peace.

Kate had heard the soft closing of the front door and guessed it was her Scotty off for a run. He was a creature of habit and always went out running when he was stressed and anxious. She smiled to herself and rose and put on her robe, which came courtesy of Sublime Retreats and was a fetching cream colour. She loved the little touches and guarantee of the standard she received from the company; it was more than worth the cost of her recent membership for that sense of security she felt travelling with them. She didn't want any surprises.

The fact that their head office was in Houston and she could pop in at any time to discuss her needs was a bonus. She had hesitated when she first walked into their plush offices as she'd been struck by how young they all were and thought of bolting out the door. But an hour later, after listening to their sales pitch and reading the brochures relating all the services that they offered throughout the many destinations that they operated in worldwide, she'd been sold, and a hefty bank transfer later meant she could now travel pretty much anywhere knowing she would be looked after all the way.

She padded out into the kitchen and made some coffee before following unknowingly in Scott's footsteps out onto the terrace to admire the amazing view. After a few minutes of blissfulness she became aware of a regular, watery sweeping sound from the direction of the pool, so, coffee in hand, she wandered over to investigate. There, perspiration already forming on his broad, now bare, muscular back, was a Greek Adonis you only read of in works of fiction. He was rhythmically skimming the surface of the pool with a long-handled net, removing any debris that had accumulated overnight. With each languid stroke, his biceps rippled, causing her to catch her breath involuntarily.

She wasn't sure how long she stood there staring at him before he became aware of her presence. He smiled as he turned, his teeth gleaming white against his sun-browned skin and, putting down the net, came up the steps to greet her. 'Kalimera. I am Thomas the pool boy and gardener for you.'

Kate caught herself; the boy was about the same age as her son, for god's sake. 'Good morning, Thomas,' she replied. 'My name is Kate. Thank you for looking after everything so well, it's beautiful. Can I offer you some refreshment?' She flinched at how prissy she sounded.

Thomas's face screwed up into a frown. 'Refreshment? What is this refreshment?' he asked, looking even younger in his confusion.

Kate laughed. 'I'm sorry, I only meant would you like a drink, some water or perhaps a coffee?' she stammered.

So, when Linda and Charlotte emerged from their bedrooms half an hour later, they found Kate in deep conversation in the kitchen with a gorgeous stranger who was making her laugh so much, tears were rolling down her face.

'Shit' hissed Charlotte, very aware of her morning hair. 'She could've warned us there was a stud lurking in the kitchen,' and she darted back downstairs to make herself presentable. Marc wandered in yawning, did a double-take at the semi-clad young man, and then ambled over to the coffee machine and started randomly pressing buttons. Linda was amazed at how animated Kate looked; the old bag looked almost girlish.

It occurred to her then that Kate had not been with, or shown interest in, another man since her husband had left as far as she was aware. It had never crossed her mind to think of Kate as someone who would have needs, someone who would be affected in the presence of an attractive member of the opposite sex.

As Kate was making introductions, Peter's head appeared around the door. 'Cooee, good morning everyone, I hope you all slept well?' he said, walking in, followed by a dumpy, dark-haired woman of indistinguishable age. 'This is Maria the maid; she will be coming in to make your breakfast every morning and generally looking after the villa.'

They all smiled and said 'good morning, Maria' dutifully and the woman nodded, avoided all eye contact, scuttled to the cupboards and got to work, rattling pots and pans as she began her preparations

'Peter, shall you and I step onto the terrace and talk through the itinerary?' Kate said, giving him a sly wink as she did so.

'I think we should all be involved in this conversation, don't you?' Linda said pointedly, making a move towards the doors.

Marc, the only other person in the room aware of the grand plans and the need for secrecy, called out, 'Linda, could you please give me a hand to work out this confounded coffee machine first? We can join them in a minute; you know I can't function until I've had some caffeine.'

Linda smiled at his lost, little boy expression and went to help, despite feeling aggrieved that Kate was yet again taking command of everything and determined to get out there and join the conversation as soon as she could.

Charlotte, who chose this moment to sashay back into the room wearing her skimpiest bikini and a see-through sarong, walked, hips swaying in time to the strains of Lady Marmalade, which she'd cued on the sound system, and approached Thomas.

'I don't think we've been introduced,' she purred to the startled looking Thomas. 'I am Charlotte, and I am very delighted to meet you.'

The poor pool boy did not know where to look and you could see his skin redden, despite his deep tan from working outside.

'I, erm, I also glad to meet you, miss Charlotte,' he stuttered, before downing the dregs of his coffee and bolting for the door.

'Well, isn't he just to die for' giggled Charlotte, realising this was her perfect opportunity to make Marc jealous.

'Leave him be,' Linda said, 'come and help Marc make his coffee while I go and check what Ms D is busily arranging on our behalf and without our blessing.'

They both watched her stomp outside, indignation oozing from every pore.

'She totally needs to chill out regarding Scott's mum,' Charlotte offered as she deftly made them both a cappuccino and took her first tentative sip.

'Yeah, especially as she's nearly her mother-in-law' Marc smirked, then slapped his hand over his mouth, eyes wide in horror as he realised what he had said. He'd been sworn to secrecy, as they all knew Charlotte would not be able to stay quiet and keep something this important from her friend. Charlotte whirled around, the motion nearly spilling her coffee.

'What are you talking about, Marc?'

'It's nothing, it's only. Oh, to hell with it, you'll find out, anyway. Scott is going to propose to Linda this week, down on the beach. Kate has arranged everything, even a photographer.'

Charlotte visibly blanched. This was bad. This was not good timing and the fact that Kate had organised it all made it a zillion times worse. But before she could say anything, Scott staggered in, dripping with sweat and bright red from the exertion of his run.

'Morning, sleepy heads, I have run for miles this morning and I feel on top of the world!' he exclaimed exuberantly. He glanced at their tense faces, sensing something was not quite right 'where's Ma and Linda?'

'They are outside with the concierge. I think it might be a good idea if you go join them, Scott, before world war three breaks out.' said Marc, and picked up his coffee. 'We'll come with you, mate', and they trooped outside to the sound of Linda's rising voice.

'I am just saying that, of course, I appreciate everything you have organised for this trip, but there must be some room for flexibility. What if I don't want to go for 'a romantic walk' with Scott along the beach at exactly noon on Thursday? Who organises things to that degree? Have you never heard of spontaneity? This is completely insane!'

Peter looked around at his guests, realising he had to do something swiftly to avert this crisis, his gaze lingering a few seconds longer than necessary on Marc before he stood up and went over to Linda.

'I think what's been lost a little in translation here,' said Peter in soothing tones, waving his clipboard with the reviled itinerary around in an attempt to lessen its importance 'is the fact that Kate thought it would be nice for you and Scott to have some alone time. She realises it can be difficult as a couple travelling with a group, especially your boyfriend's mother, and she wanted to make sure that the two of you had some space.'

Linda looked taken aback. It had never entered her mind that Kate's thinking would include anything other than a need to dominate and be in control. She glanced at Kate, then around at the rest of the group, who were all staring at her, waiting to see her response. She still didn't fancy it, but maybe it would be a good opportunity for her to talk to Scott, explain how unhappy she was feeling and perhaps tell him it was time to go their separate ways?

'Ok, fine,' she conceded anxiously, twisting her necklace. 'But Peter, you and I are going to have a talk about things *I* can do for the rest of the week should I choose to.'

'Breakfast it is ready!' called Maria, coming out onto the terrace with perfect timing and bearing a large tray weighed down with food. 'Please be seated, everybody.'

'I'm going to run and grab a quick shower' said Scott. 'You all dive in. The food looks amazing.' As they began to shuffle around and find their places at the dining table, Marc took Peter discreetly to one side.

'Well done, dude. I thought it was all going to blow up then. I owe you a drink' he said, leaning in to talk, smiling at the concierge and putting a conspiratorial arm around his shoulder, causing Peter to freeze on the spot. 'Hope you have time to join us at the restaurant on Thursday, you know, after the *thing*.'

Pulling yet again on his professional resources, Peter smiled. 'I'm sure I'll be able to spend some time with you for a while, at least. I think we'll all need a drink by then. And on that note' he said, turning and including those at the table in his statement and using the manoeuvre to duck out from under Marc's arm.

'I have a million and one things to do before our local tour this morning, including getting those gates fixed. They seem to be stuck open at the moment, so I'd better be off. If you have any problems within the house and should you be unable to reach me, the telephone numbers for both Maria and Thomas are in the villa book on the coffee table.' he said and, giving them his best smile, he headed out of the front door, his shoulders still tingling from Marc's touch.

The breakfast spread was amazing: fresh fruits, including the biggest watermelon they'd ever seen, wonderful creamy tasting Greek yoghurt and local honey, warm bread from the bakers, butter, jam and pastries. Maria crept back out, 'excuse me, can I cook some eggs for you?'

Looking around at the amount of food on the table and with an apple pie halfway to his mouth Marc said, 'well I can't speak for anyone else, but there's enough here already for me.'

'I can make any way you like,' Maria persisted, looking hopeful.

'I think we're set, Maria,' said Kate kindly. 'Maybe tomorrow we can try your eggs?'

Maria nodded and scuttled off as they loaded up their plates, piling them high with all the goodies on offer.

Scott, who'd had a quick shower and was now sitting next to Linda, placed his hand over hers on the table and whispered 'are you ok?'

'Yes, I'm fine. It will be good for us to get out, have a chat,' she said deliberately, avoiding his gaze and slipping her hand out from under his on the pretext of reaching for more bread.

Breakfast was a leisurely affair, which they lingered over, enjoying every mouthful. Putting her knife and fork together neatly on her plate and placing her napkin on top, Kate gave a contented sigh. She looked at her watch. 'I suppose we should start getting ready for Peter's grand local tour,' she said, pushing her chair back and standing up.

'Yes, especially Marc and Charlotte,' said Scott with a cheeky grin 'if we want to leave at some point today, they better get their skates on.'

'Haha, very funny,' said Charlotte, slapping him across the back of his head as she walked past. 'Come on Marc, we don't have to listen to this ridicule,' she fumed, grabbing his arm as they went inside. Kate laughed, 'come on, lovebirds, you too. We have roughly half an hour until Peter gets here,' and she followed in the other couple's footsteps.

Not wanting to be alone with Scott right now, Linda jumped up too. 'We'd better do as she says or we'll be in trouble,' she said and grinned to show it was a joke, and they both went to their rooms to get dressed.

Peter was exactly on time and he was happy to see all five of his guests standing by the front door, waiting for him. He climbed out of his car, smiling at the group. 'Right, are we ready for the local tour, everyone?'

'We certainly are. I'm sure it will be the highlight of our day,' said Marc mockingly, smiling at the concierge, who blushed.

'Would one of you like to come in my car?' said Peter, looking at him hopefully. 'To give you a little more room.'

'I will,' said Linda hastily, and walked towards the vehicle before anyone could object. She was feeling extremely claustrophobic right now, so this was the perfect opportunity to have a break from Scott and Kate, if only for a little while.

Their first port of call was the beautiful beach below the villa called Avlaki. Stony, rugged and beautiful, it was breathtaking; with just a few sunbeds and umbrellas strung along the beach, it seemed wild and uninhabited.

'This is one of my favourite places to swim' Peter was saying. 'The water here is fantastic and up at the far end there' - he pointed - 'you can walk around the headland which is a wildlife preserve, and find some gorgeous secluded swimming spots. It's also a great area for snorkelling.

They climbed back into their cars and made their way to a small roadside supermarket called Nikos, where Peter introduced them to the delightful family that owned the store that was open all day every day through the summer months.

'I have opened an account for you here,' he told them, 'so you can add any supplies you need to it throughout the week and then you can settle up at the end.' They wandered around the store, amazed at all the produce packed so cleverly into a relatively small space and admiring the fresh, home-made dips available at the deli counter. They couldn't help but giggle at the sign carefully listing in English the ingredients of each dip that declared the Taramasalata to be made from 'God roe.'

'My, my, he really does move in mysterious ways,' said Marc, sotto voiced, causing them all to explode with laughter.

Once they had finished investigating the store, they drove on another few minutes to the small harbour village of Kassiopi, a charming resort full of pretty little shops selling souvenirs, local crafts and fantastical inflatables for the pool. There was a wonderful bakery, its aroma drawing them in, where they stocked up on baklavas and an amazing orange cake, sticky with syrup, that smelt divine. They wandered down to the waterfront where they photographed the array of picturesque, multi-coloured fishing boats, draped with nets, bobbing up and down in the quay, before walking up the winding path up to the castle ruins overlooking the harbour and admiring the views from above.

'This is one of the three strategically placed castles that defended the island in times gone by and dates back to the Byzantine era, as do most of our historical monuments.' said Peter, who had spent many hours researching the history of the island. 'Tonight you are booked into that taverna on the other side of the harbour, called Tavernaki,' he advised them, pointing to the spot in the distance. 'You can drive down and park at the front there. Your table is booked for 7 o'clock.'

As they wandered back up the cobbled street through the village, Peter pointing out useful things such as the pharmacy and ATMs, the boys opted to sit and have a cold glass of Mythos beer whilst the girls did some shopping, all three of them finding something they 'absolutely' had to buy. Charlotte found some strappy gladiator style sandals which accentuated her lean legs and Kate and Linda both found pashminas they liked. Linda loved the fact that hers had a large blue eye embroidered on it that was supposed to ward off evil spirits, according to the shopkeeper.

'Maybe it will keep Kate in check,' she whispered to her friend as they left the shop, and they both giggled.

They walked back up to the car park, hot but happy. 'I'll sure be glad to get back to our lovely cool villa,' said Charlotte, fanning herself with her hand in the back seat.

'Me too' said Scott, looking at her in the rear-view mirror. 'That pool seems pretty inviting right now!'

'I think we should spend the afternoon making the most of the villa,' said Kate as they pulled into the drive and parked alongside Peter's car.

'Peter,' she called as he got out of his car and opened the door for Linda, 'we're all feeling the effects of the time difference and climate, so I think we shall spend this afternoon by the pool.'

'That is a perfect idea; you have a full day out on the boat tomorrow, so take the opportunity to relax and do nothing. You are on holiday after all!' and, with a friendly wave, he got back in his car and drove off.

'He's such a lovely guy,' said Linda, walking towards the door.

'He is, isn't he' said Marc thoughtfully, staring after the car for a moment before going inside to follow the others.

Settled around the pool, the girls were all engrossed - Kate and Linda in the novels they had brought on the trip and Charlotte busy flipping through her magazines looking at the latest fashions. The boys made a half-hearted attempt at a game of handball in the infinity pool, but when the inflatable ball went over the edge for the third time they gave up and sprawled out the sun loungers chatting, enjoying this chance to hang out together away from the usual time restraints of their normal life.

'Does anyone want a drink?' called Scott as he headed towards the kitchen.

'I'll take a glass of water,' said Linda, standing up. 'In fact, I think I'm going to lie down for a bit. I have a headache. Must be all this sun,' she added, following him inside.

'You OK, honey?' said Scott, handing her a glass, which she gratefully sipped some ice-cold water from.

'I'm sure I'll be fine. I feel just like I need to be somewhere cool and quiet for a while,' she replied, and she left him frowning and chewing his lip in concern. In the cool of her room, she smiled to herself, savouring this moment of solitude. She pulled out her laptop and was soon lost in another world, travelling to virtual promised lands and oblivious to all the problems she'd left behind.

That night's dinner was a subdued affair, despite the charming taverna with its harbour front location and candlelit tables. Linda had cried off, claiming she still had a headache and insisting Scott should go despite his protestations. His obvious concern and muted attitude affected the whole table and, try as they might, they couldn't shake him out of it.

Marc was not his usual self either; one of his favourite patients at the veterinary practice he ran had been brought in as an emergency. The elderly cat was not looking good, and he was feeling guilty for not being there for her, and kept glancing at his phone, waiting for updates on her condition.

That left Kate and Charlotte desperately trying to make small talk, even though they had absolutely nothing in common and had never really had the chance to bond.

'That's another fabulous bag, Ms D.' Charlotte said brightly. 'You seem to have a different one every time we go out.'

'It's a Balenciaga,' she said, raising her eyebrows as she fondly stroked the pale pink clutch she had brought out that night. 'My Scotty buys me a new bag every time he gets a bonus'.

Scott smiled wanly at this comment, running his hands through his hair and said, 'I should probably stop spoiling you and start saving up; I may have more important things to spend my hard-earned bucks on soon.'

They all nodded, deep within their own thoughts about the upcoming proposal and were grateful for the distraction when the waitress brought a plate of freshly cut fruit to the table to signify the end of the meal.

Back at the villa, Linda was having a grand old time by herself. With her music on full blast, she was sitting at the table on the terrace with her laptop, checking out beach huts in Sri Lanka. She'd made herself a sandwich from the leftovers of the arrival meze and was sipping on a glass of Kate's Whispering Angel, which tasted all the sweeter in this luxurious moment of solitude.

She was beginning to think that maybe she wasn't meant to be part of a couple. Well, not yet anyway. Perhaps she really should travel the world before settling down? It was a scary but exhilarating thought, and one she fully intended to talk through with Scott on Thursday. When she received a message from him letting her know they were on their way back to the villa, she hastily cleared away the signs of her solitary party and quickly went to her room so she could pretend to be asleep when they got back.

WEDNESDAY

The day dawned bright and blue yet again, promising a perfect day for the boat trip. As agreed, Peter was at the house a little before 9 am to show them the way down to San Stefano where they were to meet Captain Yiannis on board his 30-foot motor yacht, Nafsica.

As they drove, taking each bend with care, down towards the coast on a road that snaked its way through the olive groves, a picture-perfect bay was revealed between the trees, the sea gleaming and glinting in the horseshoe-shaped cove below.

'My God, this place is stunning,' Scott exclaimed, gazing down at the bay. 'I always thought the pictures I'd seen of Corfu were photoshopped but the colours are truly amazing.'

Linda, who had decided to make a real effort today to join in, nodded and said 'it is beautiful, thanks again Kate for organising all this.' Scott, who sat next to her in the car, smiled gratefully and squeezed her hand.

They parked the car in the shade below a cluster of trees and walked around to the waterfront, lined with tavernas which all had jetties busy with small boats, Peter leading the way.

'There he is' said Peter, and led them through one of the tavernas laid out for breakfast service on to the jetty at the end of which was tied a smart, two-tiered, blue and white boat.

Looking up from tying a bowline and seeing them approaching, a tall, dark-haired man who looked to be in his early fifties jumped off the side, his arms open wide in greeting.

'Hello, hello, I am Captain Yiannis! Welcome to my boat, Nafsica. We are going to have a fantastic day!' he declared, smiling in welcome at his guests. His enthusiasm was contagious and, after they had all introduced themselves, they clambered on board as fast as they could, handing their bags of beach towels and sun creams ahead, eager to be off. His deckhand Manolis pulled in the fenders and the bowlines and they were soon motoring away from the pretty harbour and out to sea.

Peter stood on the jetty, waving them off, heartily wishing he could join them. Marc was looking particularly dashing today and the thought of him emerging from the sea in his trunks was making him feel quite light-headed. With a sigh, he dragged himself away and walked back to his car to return to the office to catch up on his paperwork. Knowing his guests were in very good hands and wouldn't be returning until after 5 pm meant he had a full day free from his obligations to them.

When he walked into the office, Emma looked up from her computer and smiled. 'Morning, gorgeous. How's life treating you?' she said as he walked over to the kitchen area to grab some coffee.

'Pretty good I guess, can't complain' he smiled back at her, but she could see a flicker of something in his eyes that wasn't quite right.

'What's up with you?' she said, getting up with her empty mug for a top-up. Her ability to down coffee all day was legendary in the office, as were her man-eating tendencies.

Looking around to make sure that no one was earwigging, he said, 'you know the Delaney party that I have in the villa right now?'

'Yes, of course,' said Emma, all ears, anticipating a juicy morsel of gossip like the sex toy wielding couple of last month.

'Well, one of them, his name's Marc.'

'Yes, yes, spit it out man, what's with this Marc?'

'Well, he's gorgeous.'

Emma stared at Peter, her disappointment over the lack of gossip quickly being replaced by the realisation her friend was trying to tell her something. She was aware that he was looking for love and knew all about the app he'd downloaded. They'd spent many an hour in local bars giggling at some of the more insane profiles and trying to guess who it was close by that was showing up on there, but she had never held out much hope of him meeting someone decent through it.

'So, what's the deal? Do you think he's into you?'

'That's the thing,' said Peter, looking downcast. 'He's straight, a real womaniser, by all accounts. I can't believe the first guy I fancy in years is off-limits.'

Emma gave her friend a hug. 'Never mind, hun. There is without question someone out there for you. Someone gorgeous and kind and as crazy about cats as you are... But, in the meantime, do you think you could set me up with this guy, Marc?'

'You can go off people you know,' he said, laughing, and, feeling a little better about the world, went to sit at his desk and get on with his day.

Onboard the Nafsica, things were going with a swing. With traditional Greek music playing in the background, they were all relaxing and enjoying the atmosphere.

‘Come on, everyone’ called the captain, pouring large measures of clear liquid from an unmarked bottle into plastic cups. ‘It is traditional for us to start the day with this,’ he said, handing them round.

'What is it?' said Kate, sniffing it suspiciously. The overpowering aniseed smell hitting her sinuses. Charlotte, who'd taken a big swig, choked, tears streaming down her face. 'My God, it's rocket fuel,' she laughed, wiping her eyes.

‘We can add a little water to it if you find it too strong,’ said Manolis, proffering a bottle to her.

‘Nah, I’m good, honey,’ she said, downing the rest of her drink.

‘I’ll take some,’ said Kate, who’d been sipping a little more sedately, and held out her cup.

‘This is Ouzo, the national drink of Greece and the backbone of our country,’ declared captain Yiannis, and poured himself another generous measure.

As the yacht motored along the coast and the wind cooled their faces, Linda beamed with joy. Experiences similar to this, so remote from her usual life, were exactly what she had been dreaming of. Never mind that Kate had organised this and the weight of the conversation she knew she was going to have with Scott tomorrow. She was determined to make the most of every single moment.

As they meandered down the dramatic coast, its craggy rock face sweeping down to meet the sea in small coves and beaches, the captain pointed out all the sights. The Rothschild Estate lording castle-like above Kerasia and a regular haunt of Prince Charles and Camilla, Prospero’s cell and The White House of Laurence Durrell fame and, slowing down so they could admire, the superyachts they passed, moored haughtily in the bays demanding attention from all that saw them.

They pulled up to anchor and swam through some narrow-mouthed caves; the girls squealing in alarm when they disturbed some bats and splashing crazily to make a speedy exit, making the men laugh out loud at their efforts. They stopped again, further up the coast, by the rugged Kapereli Island, home to the small lighthouse marking the entrance to the narrow channel that ran between Corfu and the mainland. Captain Yiannis pointed to the ledge on one side. 'OK, from there you can jump,' he said casually, and they all looked in amazement. 'Come on boys; don't make me have to show you how it's done.' He laughed at their anxious faces.

Scott and Marc reluctantly climbed off the boat and swam over to the small shingle beach below the ledge. Charlotte dived gracefully over the side, and after swimming a circuit of the island, followed them. The boys stood on the ledge looking down into the water, neither too keen on the idea of leaping off.

'After you,' said Marc, grinning nervously at Scott who shrank back a little at the thought and was opening his mouth to respond when the air was split with a loud whoop and Charlotte came barrelling past and leapt straight off the edge without hesitation.

The sound of Linda and Kate's laughter echoing up from the boat gave them the push they needed, and they both threw themselves over, yelling all the way down. When they climbed back on board, their faces were flushed with the adrenalin rush and they accepted the girls, teasing them with good grace.

Manolis, ever attendant, provided them with a constant supply of drinks as the day went on; wine from the captain's vineyard for the girls and beers for the boys, whilst the captain regaled them with stories of local life. It was an idyllic day, and they were all feeling more carefree than they had in a long time.

As it approached lunchtime, they motored back up the coast a short distance, anchored in a secluded bay, and the captain flipped open the BBQ on the back of the boat. Soon the air was filled with amazing, tantalising smells. The girls lay on the front of the boat sunbathing while Kate chatted away with captain Yiannis as he cooked and learnt more about his way of life, and the boys took turns diving off the side to retrieve various items from the depths with their newfound courage.

'This is bliss' Linda said to her friend as they dozed contentedly on the sun deck at the front of the boat, reddening in the strong July sun despite the layers of sun cream. Her eyes were closed, and she was feeling drowsy, the sound of the water gently licking the side of the boat making her completely relaxed and unable to move to apply some more factor 50, even though she knew she should.

'I could do this every day, that's for sure,' Charlotte replied, smiling up at the sky and adjusting her hat to provide more shade to her face, which was beaded with perspiration.

She sat up to accept yet another glass of cold white wine from Manolis, her elbow knocking the book she'd carelessly abandoned on the side into the water in the process. Without a word the boy dived in after it, retrieving it before it had time to start sinking and held it aloft for her to take and then agilely clambered, dripping, back on board.

'Thank you so much, I was getting to the good bit!' Charlotte said, laying the book out in the sun to dry and rewarding him with a brilliant smile. The young man flushed and was thinking about how to respond when Marc walked up to call them for lunch. Charlotte's attention was at once laser-focused on Marc and she leapt up to follow him, brushing past Manolis without another thought.

They all seated themselves around the table after collecting plates and cutlery, eagerly anticipating the feast that, by the smells they'd been enduring for the last hour, was going to be incredible.

The food started coming thick and fast, huge slabs of fresh bread, Greek salad with salty feta and juicy tomatoes from the captain's garden, spicy tzatziki with enough garlic to blow your head off and grilled Saganaki drenched in fresh lemon juice. They all greedily started to load up their plates, exclaiming in delight with every mouthful, each new taste a revelation.

The captain walked through bearing a large platter and, with a flourish, placed it on the table in front of them. 'Here you are, the best-mixed seafood plate you will find in Greece,' he announced proudly.

Five pairs of eyes looked down at the magnificent platter, two of which were horrified.

Laden with octopus, shrimps, oysters and small fish and decorated with lemon slices and fresh parsley, it was splendid, so it was unfortunate that it was due to become the cause of an almighty explosion.

'What the hell is this?!' demanded Linda, glaring at Kate, her face infused with anger. Scott jumped up, holding out his hands, trying to calm her down.

'I'm sure Ma has ordered something else for you,' he said, glancing at Kate and hoping for reassurance.

Kate paled. 'I'm sorry, Linda, I didn't think. I'm sure the lovely Captain can fix you something else up.'

Captain Yiannis, who didn't understand what the problem was but realised he was expected to produce something else, said, 'I am sorry madam Kate, I have onboard only what you ordered.'

'I can't believe that you've done this again' spluttered Linda, slamming a fist on the table. 'Three years on and you're still pulling this shit, treating me as if I don't exist!'

With that, she pushed the platter away from her, causing a deluge of food-laden plates and cutlery on the other side of the table to hit the deck with a resounding crash, stood up and stormed off back to the front of the boat.

'Well,' Charlotte said, whilst wiping at the debris that had landed on her lap, managing to smear more of it than clean it. 'That's not good'. Manolis instantly ran up with a roll of kitchen paper for her, standing by, unsure of what else to do while she tried to clean herself up, dabbing at the oily salad dressing running down her legs and picking bits of tomato and cucumber off her shorts.

Kate looked at Scott in trepidation, 'I'm sorry, Scotty, I didn't mean to upset her, I only wanted you to have your favourite foods and make today perfect for you'. Scott shook his head in despair, his face a picture of wretchedness as his eyes darted between the catastrophe that had been lunch, and the direction Linda had gone.

'Ma, I know you always have my best interests at the forefront of everything that you do, but you know what would make this day perfect for me? Linda being happy. That's all I want, the girl I love with me and both of us having a perfect day. The sooner you get that into your head and start paying attention to her needs, the better.' And with that, he valiantly followed in Linda's angry footsteps. Charlotte, looking up from where she was knelt, helping Manolis clean up the ruins of the meal on the floor, said to Kate,

'Ms D, you really have put your foot in it this time. Once she has calmed her down, I think you'd better go and apologise to her big time. She's madder than a wet hen!'

'I'm sure she will be fine,' said Kate, smiling and pushing her chin out. 'After tomorrow everything will be perfect'. Kate felt bad for upsetting the girl yet again, but she knew Linda would be ecstatic tomorrow when Scott asked her to be his wife - why wouldn't she? - And then all this nonsense would be forgotten.

Marc stood looking on, worried for his friend and the relationship he was pinning so much on. He had seen Linda's face as she stormed by him and he didn't hold out much hope of Scott calming her down any time soon.

'I'm not sure he will be able to calm her down. In fact, the chances are slim to none, and slim done got up and left.' he said, trying and failing to make a joke out of the situation.

On the prow of the boat, things were not going well. Scott had tried to embrace Linda but had been pushed forcefully and pointedly away.

'Linda, please don't take Ma's actions to heart. She doesn't mean to upset you,' he said, pacing up and down a safe distance from her. She looked angry enough to make him walk the plank.

'She doesn't think about me full stop. I'm just an accessory like those damn handbags she insists on toting around.'

She glared at him; her face flushing, daring him to deny this, but he purely stopped pacing and stood looking helplessly at her.

'We need to talk about this, Scott; I can't bear the way she behaves. I think her idea of a "romantic walk" tomorrow,' she said with sarcastic emphasis, 'will be a good opportunity for us to set things straight. Talk over things without the others around.'

Scott smiled at her, a shred of hope in his mind. Yes, tomorrow he could explain everything and then pop the question and Linda would understand that she meant everything to him, no matter how his mother behaved.

'That's a great idea, sweetheart; we can set everything straight tomorrow.'

The rest of the day passed, unsurprisingly, with a strained atmosphere. Charlotte made up a large plate of everything but seafood to take to Linda, who steadfastly refused to move from her position at the front of the boat. Scott was barely talking to his mum and had gone up to the upper sun deck. Unfortunately, he had forgotten his hat and the sun cream, so was suffering as he slowly burnt until he had the sense to message Marc and ask him to bring his bag up. Marc appeared a few minutes later and tossed his bag to him. 'I've brought you some water as well,' he said, grinning at his friend's reddening face.

'I could do with something a little stronger,' Scott replied but drank a few gulps of the refreshing cold water, anyway.

Marc handed him a bottle of beer. 'What would you do without me?' he said while popping his bottle with a hiss and passing the opener to Scott.

'I really don't know. You've always been there for me, mate. I don't think I tell you enough how much I appreciate the fact that I can share anything with you,' Scott said, placing his beer to one side and digging his sun cream and hat out of his bag. Marc sat contemplatively for a while, watching the wash behind the boat.

'That's the thing with friends; you should be able to tell them anything, right?'

'Of course,' Scott paused mid application of the cream; 'although I don't need to tell you what's up right now,' he grinned sheepishly. 'I figure it's pretty damn obvious.'

'Yes, that's true,' Marc laughed. 'I don't envy you right now for sure. But I was trying to say we should be able to tell each other anything, anytime, and know that the other would be there for them.'

Scott looked at his friend, who was still staring out to sea and avoiding eye contact. 'Marc, you know I will always have your back, whatever happens. But right now, I need to focus on getting through tomorrow and making things right with Linda. After that, we can discuss your... Well, whatever it is you're hesitating to tell me, ok?'

Marc stood and patted his friend on the back. 'Sure thing, dude, it'll keep. And now I better go back down and check on Charlotte and your mum. The poor captain looked terrified last time I saw him!' and with that, he swung himself back down the stairs to the lower deck.

Poor captain Yiannis was working twice as hard as usual to entertain them all. Normally by this stage in the afternoon, he could take a break from being host; his guests would be sleeping off their food and ouzo at this point. But instead, he was having to redouble his efforts to entertain them, blasting out Abba songs in an effort to lighten the mood as they motored back to San Stefano to disembark earlier than planned.

Luckily, they hadn't booked to go out for dinner that night. Peter had advised them not to, as he knew after the gargantuan feast provided on the boat, as a rule, his guests could not face another meal the same day. Having returned to the villa, Linda was making use of the office and losing herself in another world. A world of travel and adventure where bossy old maids didn't exist, and she was free to eat whatever the hell she liked.

Charlotte and Kate were sharing the space around the pool, both of them too tired to bother trying to pretend that the day had gone well, and were lying in easy silence on their sunbeds, soaking up the last of the day's sun.

Marc strolled around the grounds until he found his friend, who had disappeared as soon as they had returned. He was sitting in one of the secluded areas where the only sound was the gentle susurration of the pools overflow, holding something in his hands and looking downhearted.

'Cheer up, it might not happen,' he called blithely, announcing his presence and waving the after sun lotion he'd brought at Scott, whose now scarlet face needed some attention.

'That's what I'm afraid of,' said Scott, opening his hand and revealing the ring he'd held, clasped so tight it had left indentations in his palm. The sun struck the enormous diamond, reflecting beams of light around him and casting a halo of colours.

'Wow, that is one hunk of rock,' said Marc, taking it from him as he sat down and, passing him the lotion, marvelling at the beauty of the ring before placing it on the table between them. Scott snatched it up and held it close, the lotion bottle falling unheeded into his lap.

'Settle down, Frodo!' said Marc, who had become more concerned about his friend's obsession with the thing as the week had progressed. 'You would be better off putting that in the safe in your room.'

'I can't let it out of my sight. I somehow feel if I don't keep it with me it will be bad luck and she'll say no.' Scott replied, gripping it firmly again.

'I think we both know that is complete nonsense. I never had you down as superstitious.'

'I'm not. It's simply because this is so damn important. I'm as nervous as hell despite Ma's planning, or maybe because of it... It's almost as if I have to make two women happy tomorrow.'

Marc looked at Scott with concern. 'Are you sure you want to do this?' he asked, at last broaching a subject that had been playing on his mind. 'It seems to me that your mum wants this to happen more than you do, and it's not something that you should go into with any doubts.'

'It might not be my idea of how to pop the question but, as for the actual question itself, I am in no doubt at all,' said Scott, looking positive for the first time in days. 'I love Linda with all my heart and her becoming my wife is everything I could wish for.'

'Well, in that case, forget about your mum and everyone else and let Linda know this tomorrow. That's all she needs to hear. Now put some of that cream on your face or nobody will want to marry you!'

THURSDAY

The next day, as the others pretended to get ready for some more sunbathing by the pool, Scott and Linda put on some sensible walking shoes to make their way down to the beach below.

'We'll meet you two later at the taverna and don't forget to take some water,' Kate called from the terrace as they walked towards the door.

'Yes, Ma,' Scott replied, obediently trotting back to the kitchen to pick up a couple of small bottles and placing them in his bag, absently patting the side pocket as he did so.

Linda knew then and there that she had to do it. She had to tell Scott how she felt. There was a block of ice in the pit of her stomach at the thought. It was the worst timing possible, but she couldn't keep all her feelings, all her doubts, to herself a day longer. She was going to have to let him down gently.

Making sure that the couple had gone far enough away not to be able to hear her, Kate called out to Marc and Charlotte, who were by the pool.

'Come on, ya'll get dressed, you two. Peter has organised a taxi to come and pick us up in a minute and take us to the restaurant so we can watch the big event!' she said excitedly, her eyes glowing in anticipation.

It was then that the full plan was explained to Charlotte, including the extra guests that would be there as witnesses, and she was horrified. As she and Marc came up from the pool, she put her hand on his arm to stop him on the stairs.

'I have a bad feeling about this. Linda is really not in a good place regarding the relationship right now. Do you think we should try to warn Scott?'

Marc looked at her, concern on his face. 'There's not much we can do now, Lotte. They've already left and the Ms D. action plan is in full swing. All we can do is keep our fingers crossed and hope it ends well,' he said and bounded up the stairs towards the villa to get dressed.

Peter was at the restaurant putting up the balloons he'd chosen in tones of aqua and blue and arranging the flowers at suitable intervals on the long table that the staff had prepared for the party. They had organised the table under the wooden gazebo structure near the front, looking out to the peacock shaded sea.

He looked around, admiring the way they had, in stages, built up the seating area over the years. From the raised deck and built-in seat surrounding the enormous Plane tree that provided shade for part of the garden, which was lit up at night he knew with fairy lights, to the meandering crazy paved path that led into the main building, punctuated with terracotta pots wound with rope and bursting with colourful flowers, they had managed to create a charming, peaceful oasis, with pockets of private dining areas, despite how busy they always got throughout the season.

He'd received a text from Lucy to say she was running a little late but had plenty of time, and he had called Vasso at the hotel reception to check that the gang staying there was ready to leave. The plan was to get them inside the restaurant before Scott and Linda walked up the beach. The timing was everything. He looked at his watch; there was still half an hour until Scott would lead

Linda onto the jetty, so he had time for a Freddo, his favourite cold coffee. He waved at Virgil the waiter and placed his order before going to sit at the front where tables and chairs were looking onto the beach, so he could keep an eye out.

Ten minutes later, he saw a group of people coming up the road from the direction of the hotel. 'This is it' he thought to himself, 'showtime!' He gathered the elderly group together and led them, chattering, into the restaurant at the same time that the taxi bearing Kate, Charlotte and Marc pulled up. Everyone hurried inside and took up positions where they could see the jetty clearly without being seen.

Peter looked at the time. Where was Lucy? There was barely 15 minutes to go. He ran out onto the road, then ran along the seafront, looking up and down. There was no sign of movement from the direction of the bus stop but, turning around, there in the distance he could see a couple of figures. Scott and Linda...shit! He tried calling Lucy's number, but the recorded message said the phone was out of range; he then tried her sister's number in case she was using that one, but that was switched off. Hell, what was he going to do? Ten more minutes and the couple would be on the jetty and the moment would be missed. Beads of sweat started to drip down his back.

He ran back into the restaurant and was frantically looking around for inspiration when Lucy called him back.

'Where the hell are you?' he demanded.

'Whoa, fella, what's the emergency?' said Lucy in such a nonchalant tone it drove his blood pressure through the roof. 'I've just got off the bus, we've got ages yet'.

'We have not got ages yet, we've got approximately 5 minutes,' Peter retaliated, annunciating every word in the hope of getting through to her brain.

'What are you talking about? There's an hour before the shoot.'

Peter realised instantly that his ditzy photographer was on Albanian time and hardly on this planet. Grabbing Virgil the waiter as he was rushing by, he pushed a €20 note into his hand and said 'you, get on your bike, go pick up the stupid photographer from the bus stop, NOW!'

Virgil took one look at Peter's face, thrust the note into his trouser pocket, ran outside, and leapt onto his motorbike without a word. Looking back up the beach, Peter saw the couple in the distance had stopped walking and were pointing to something out at sea.

'Stay there, keep looking,' he muttered to himself, his ears straining desperately to hear the sound of the bike returning. At precisely the moment the couple turned and started to walk towards the jetty again, he heard it roaring down the road and, sweating with relief, he ran back down the side of the restaurant to meet it.

Dragging Lucy and her camera bag unceremoniously off the back of the bike, he hustled her in and through to the front of the restaurant where she would have a perfect view of the proposal.

On the beach, Scott and Linda had both been quiet, each working up the courage for what they had to say. It was a beautiful bay. Despite the beach being stony, the water was an incredible colour, various shades of turquoise, and sheltered by cliffs either end making it a real sun trap, so they were both feeling warm despite the gentle breeze.

'Water looks pretty inviting,' said Linda, fanning her face with her hand. 'Look at that yacht over there'. They paused and admired the majestic sailboat cutting through the water, both of them thinking of how they were going to start the conversation they needed to have.

'Let's go and walk to the end of that jetty,' Scott said, looking nervous and unsure. Linda looked at him thoughtfully and nodded her assent. They continued to walk towards the weathered wooden jetty. As they mounted it and began to walk along it, Linda said, 'Scott, we need to talk.'

'We do, Linda,' he replied. 'I have something I want to say to you'. He took her hand to guide her over the uneven, roughened planks near the end, his other hand reaching into his bag. Linda took a deep breath. 'Let me go first, Scott.' She paused and then blurted out, 'I'm not sure we should be together anymore.'

There, she'd said it. A wave of relief rushed over her, the block of ice in her stomach melting away as the words came out of her mouth. Scott, who had been so concentrated on getting his courage up to pop the question, took a second to process what she'd said. When it sunk in, he stumbled and fell to his knees, Linda putting a hand on his shoulder to help steady him, as he was perilously close to the edge.

In the restaurant, the excitement was mounting. 'This is it, this is it,' Kate shouted with glee.

Lucy was clicking away with gusto, zooming in to see their faces at the blissful moment. Peter, who stood nearby, was on tenterhooks. This was the event they'd all been working towards, the culmination of so much work.

Charlotte looked at the scene. She didn't know what it was. Maybe it was their posture, but something didn't feel quite right.

She glanced across at Marc and, by the look on his face, he clearly had the same idea, and he frowned at her in concern.

Scott looked up at Linda, his face etched with confusion and pain.

'Why, Linda? I love you. I want to marry you and spend my life with you.'

His words shocked her and pulled her heart to shreds. She did love him; she knew she did. 'I love you too, Scotty. But I'm not sure if I love you enough to take on you and your mum. I need some space. I know this isn't the ideal place for this, but I needed to let you know how I feel. How I've been feeling for a while now.'

He rose slowly to his feet, his gaze never leaving hers. 'Well, if space is what you need, then take it. I know how difficult my mother can be and I know you find the situation hard to deal with. I want us to work on this together, but you need to be sure about us.'

They wrapped their arms around each other, silent tears falling, and they stood there for what felt like a long time.

'Thank you, Scott, this means the world to me,' she said, pulling away and wiping her face on her arm. 'I won't join you for lunch at the taverna' she glanced across to the building. 'It looks pretty busy in there. I think I'll go back up to the villa if you don't mind, and leave you to explain this to the others.'

He nodded and, through blurry eyes, watched her as she walked back to the road before steeling himself to face his mother. In the taverna, it had fallen quiet. After the initial whoops and cries of excitement, the sense of disaster looming settled over the crowd. They all watched as Scott made his way dejectedly along the jetty, over the beach and across the road to where they were waiting. Kate was the first to move, running out to meet her son.

'Scotty, what's wrong? Where is Linda going? We have a party organised to celebrate.'

When he looked up and took in the scene inside the taverna, the table set for twenty, the balloons and flowers, the faces that he was not expecting to see, Uncle Joe waving uncertainly at him from the corner of the room, his face hardened.

'Ma, I love you, but your constant interfering has driven away the woman I love. There isn't going to be any celebration today. If I'm lucky one day there will be, but I am absolutely positive that you will have nothing to do with it!' And with that, he turned and walked off up the road, unsure where he was going to but certain he needed to get away from his mother.

Kate was devastated. Not only had all her plans gone wrong, but her son, her darling boy, had looked at her as if he hated her. She never in a million years had imagined that this day was possible. She took a moment to compose herself, then walked back, head held high, into the taverna.

'I'm afraid we won't be celebrating an engagement today,' she announced. 'It would appear that the stars of this show need a little time to sort things out.' She paused, looking around at all her friends and family, then she smiled. 'But there's no reason for us not to eat, drink and be merry. I am so very grateful to you all for making this journey here today and I am truly thankful, so bring out the champagne!' She figured she might as well take control of one part of today's events.

Marc watched Kate, wonderment playing across his face. He was so impressed by her reserve. He'd always known she was a strong woman, but he hadn't realised how strong until today. He turned to Charlotte, who was looking shell-shocked. 'Do you think

I should go after Scott?' he ventured, looking up the road after the dejected figure of his friend.

She slowly shook her head. 'I think both our friends need some time alone right now. What I think *we* should do is sit down and have some damn champagne' she smiled mischievously at him.

'You are probably right on both counts', he laughed, and they went to join the shindig that was beginning to take place at the over-decorated table.

Peter stood to one side, unsure what to do now that everything had gone wrong. He was astounded at Kate's ability to turn this disaster into a party, but that's exactly what was happening. The champagne had been cracked open and the whole family seemed to be getting into the spirit of things. Marc called to him and waved him over to where he was sitting.

'You may as well have that drink now' he said, smiling up at him in a way that made his head spin, but he sat down anyway and grabbed a glass and it was soon filled with champagne and he was sucked into the lively conversation flying around the table.

Lucy, who'd finished packing away her equipment, sauntered over to him. 'What's the deal, Petey? Am I still gonna get paid or what? And what the hell shall I do with all these shots? I'm kinda guessing they're not gonna want them!'

For some reason, Peter found this funny, and he started to laugh. It could have been the alcohol, or maybe the closeness of Marc. 'Sit down and have a drink with us, Lucy. I guarantee you will be paid. As for the pictures, I'd guess you can delete them.'

Back at the villa, Linda sat out on the terrace feeling like a huge weight had been lifted off her shoulders. But why she also felt the need to cry, she didn't quite understand. The tears hadn't stopped falling since she left Scott on the jetty. She had considered the option of packing up and leaving for a while. There was enough in her 'possibility pot' to get her home, or anywhere she fancied for that matter, but she decided that would make the situation worse.

She and Scott's lives were so intertwined. They needed to find a way to be friends, to be comfortable in the same room, and that was not going to happen unless she faced it. She realised with a start that she should send Charlotte a message. Her friend was probably worried sick about her and she hadn't even considered letting her know what was going on.

Charlotte was far from worried sick. In fact, she was having such a good time that she felt a flicker of guilt when Linda's message popped up.

All ok, I'm at the villa, see you later. L xx.

'Well, that's just fine then,' she thought through her champagne-fuelled haze, and happily draped herself back over Marc, topping up his glass as she did so. Marc looked at her, wondering how he could let her down without causing a scene. He'd always known that she fancied him but she was so not right for him on so many levels, it was never going to happen.

He turned to Peter, who was still sitting next to him; in fact, they had been getting along like a house on fire for the last few hours. 'I think we will need a taxi soonish,' he said, grinning and looking down at Charlotte, who was reapplying her lip gloss, meaningfully. Peter's heart sagged. He and Marc had been hitting it off so well, a small spark of hope had begun to burn in him that maybe the guy was interested in him. 'I need to get this lady home to bed,' Marc added, putting the nail in the coffin as far as Peter was concerned.

'Leave it with me,' said Peter, digging out his phone and calling the local taxi firm. Once he'd confirmed that the car was on its way, Peter stood and wended his way through the tables into the main body of the taverna on the pretext of going to the bathroom and slipped, unnoticed, out of the side door. He couldn't bear to see that girl all over Marc a minute longer. He knew he was being stupid, but it made him feel miserable and alone.

He messaged Emma as he left, telling her to meet him for a drink at one of their regular haunts down the coast. He was going to need a beer or two tonight to get over this engagement drama and his unrequited love. It had been one hell of a day.

Marc looked around for Peter as the taxi pulled in to thank him, but he was nowhere in sight. "Oh well, I'll catch him tomorrow," he thought as he poured Charlotte into the back of the Mercedes. He said their goodbyes to everybody, assuring Kate he would tell the taxi to come back down in an hour for her, and climbed into the car.

As they sat in the back seat, Charlotte leaned over and tried to kiss him. He grabbed her chin and moved her face away, having to be more and more forceful as she became more and more insistent in her drunken state.

'Charlotte stop, I don't want to kiss you' he said, pushing her away and back into her half of the seat.

'Don't worry about taking advantage of me,' she slurred. 'I totally give my consent,' and she lunged again.

Firmly taking her by the shoulders, shaking her and looking into her eyes, he told her, 'I do not fancy you, Charlotte. I never have and I never will, so get that into your head' and pushed her away. She sat, speechless, staring out of the window until they arrived back at the villa, where she jumped out of the car and ran through the front door. 'Shit,' he thought to himself. 'God, I hope she doesn't remember this in the morning.'

Inside the villa, Charlotte looked around for Linda, but there was no sign. She must have gone to bed already. Her glance slid over the villa book on the coffee table and a plan popped straight into her sozzled brain. She'd show that Marc, saying he didn't fancy her like she was unattractive or something. She grabbed the book and ran downstairs with it, flipping feverishly through the pages until she found the staff contact page.

She grabbed her mobile out of her bag and started to type,

Hi Thomas, this is Charlotte at the villa. I would love to spend the night with you. I will leave my shutters open for you

and hit the send button before she could change her mind. Mission accomplished, she opened her shutters then went and draped herself seductively on her bed to wait for the gorgeous Thomas. She was asleep within minutes.

Peter met Emma at a bar bizarrely called the Red Penguin in the resort of Dassia, near to where she lived. They had stumbled upon it by accident a couple of summers ago when the intense August heat had driven them in search of a cold beer. It wasn't the kind of place they would usually have picked; in fact, they had both driven past it many times but, on that glorious day, they discovered the coldest beer in Corfu. When the jovial owner set down two frosted glasses in front of them that day containing beer so cold it was similar to a slush puppy, they knew they had found their Valhalla.

So they sat there now, nursing their beers and letting the cold glasses drip condensation over their overheated limbs as they cooled down.

'You will not believe the day I've had,' said Peter after his first mouthful.

'Mine has been an adventure too,' Emma said, grinning at him. 'I found a donkey.'

'For God's sake, not more animals. Your house must look like a petting zoo by now! Who do you think you are, Mrs Durrell?'

'Not far off, I've got enough kids too so I'm nearly there, except my husband didn't die. He buggered off back to Blighty!' She laughed again before taking another swig of her beer and swatting ineffectually at a mosquito. 'Bloody mozzies are rampant tonight.'

'Well, my amazingly planned "moment" went to hell in a handcart.' Peter said, shaking his head sadly and slapping at the bug that had landed on his thigh. 'The wife-to-be said no and disappeared into the sunset. The husband-to-be also disappeared in the other direction, and the love of my life buggered off back to the villa with that floozy in tow. I'm destined to be single forever!' he sighed dramatically.

Emma laughed again at his histrionics. 'Stop being so over the top. The zero engagement wasn't your fault, you planned everything perfectly, and if that Marc fancies floozies, you're better off without him. Message back that gorgeous George on your app thingy and then I tell you what, let's go clubbing to celebrate,' she said, standing up and downing the last of her pint.

'Celebrate? What the hell are we celebrating?' said Peter, following suit and picking up his phone.

'Well, we need to wet the donkey's head,' she cackled, and they left arm in arm.

FRIDAY

The next morning Kate was up early, despite her head feeling as if a chimpanzee was playing drums inside it, and made her way into the kitchen. Wrapping the bathrobe tightly around herself, she popped a couple of painkillers and drank a large glass of water while the coffee machine heated up.

She saw a figure walk past the window and down the steps towards the pool and figured in was Thomas doing his morning duties. 'I'll take a coffee down for him,' she thought, debating whether she wanted to freshen up before doing so but deciding she didn't care what he thought she looked like.

Padding quietly down the stairs to the pool with the cup balanced carefully on a saucer she called out 'Kalimera, I have some coffee for you' startling the shabby-looking man standing there, who, as he spun around, Kate realised was plainly not Thomas.

'Are you the Putana that has been scaring my boy?!' he demanded, jabbing a finger as he strode towards her. His ferocity and visible anger caused Kate to shriek and drop the coffee. The cup smashed into a hundred pieces, splattering espresso over the limestone stairs and the edges of her cream robe.

'Look what you've made me do,' she shouted at him. 'I don't know who you are or what you are talking about, but there is no reason to speak to a lady like that!' She stood, hands-on-hips, glaring at him, shaking with indignation. Unexpectedly, his face broke into a broad smile, attractive laughter lines appearing around his intense brown eyes.

'I think you must have Greek blood in your veins to shout at a man this way,' he said and started to chuckle. He stepped forward and put out his hand. 'I apologise. My name is Pericles, and I am Thomas' father.'

As she looked at him, Kate could see the resemblance now, the broad back and the still strong arms and the handsome face that was smiling at her, and she became conscious again of what a fright she must look after the excesses of yesterday.

'I suggest that I go and make some more coffee while you clear this mess up' she indicated the coffee stains and shattered ceramic, 'and then you can explain to me exactly what this is all about.'

A short time later, Kate having quickly dressed and run a brush through her hair, they were sitting at the small table by the pool watching the swallows swoop gracefully down to collect bugs off the surface.

'So tell me, what has happened to Thomas?' said Kate, sipping her cappuccino and trying not to stare at the man sitting opposite her.

'He received some kind of message late last night. He wouldn't tell me exactly what it said, only that a lady from the villa had sent it and he did not want to come to work because of it.' He placed his cup back on the table and looked at her intently. 'I can only guess that it was of a sexual nature.'

Kate flushed slightly. 'Well, it certainly wasn't me! And I am damn sure it wouldn't have been Linda, so that leaves one person who'd do something of this nature. Do you have the number?'

He nodded slowly and pulled out a scrap of paper torn from a receipt out of his trouser pocket. On the back was scrawled a number. She picked up her phone and scrolled through her contacts to check, but she knew the answer before she reached the C's. 'What was the girl playing at' she thought to herself as she put her phone back down.

'What I don't understand' said Kate, thoughtfully sipping her coffee, 'is why Thomas is so freaked out that he feels he can't come to work. I mean Charlotte is a real looker, she has more curves than a barrel of snakes, you'd think he would be flattered.' She put down her cup and looked at Pericles, feeling slightly mesmerised by his eyes.

'Ah, I think the fault for that lies at my door,' he began, staring out to sea. 'You see, his mother left us when he was small. She... she ran off with another man, a younger man, a malakas ouzo salesman.' He took his time but continued, 'you must understand I was heartbroken, humiliated, and I was so angry all the time for many years. Thomas has grown up listening to me say "women are bad, women are devious, never trust a woman" and things of that nature. So now my poor boy does exactly that and runs every time a girl even looks at him.'

Kate, who had sat silently listening to his story which resonated so deeply inside her, laid her hand on his arm, which was resting on the table.

'You would be surprised at how much I understand. I have just driven a wedge between my son and his girlfriend, all because I couldn't let go. I felt I always had to protect him, ever since his father left us.'

As she smiled softly at him, Pericles felt something he'd sworn he'd never feel again: a stirring in his heart. He looked at her wonderingly and asked, 'Would you care to have dinner with me tonight?'

When she waved him off in his battered Fiat Punto later that morning, Kate was amazed at the turn of events. She had never expected to meet another man who could light her up inside the way her husband had, yet this local village man had sparked something in her and she had found herself agreeing to go out for dinner with him. She wandered in a daze back into the villa, her mind abuzz and a smile playing about her lips and, selecting her playlist from Bizet's Carmen, went to have some breakfast.

As Pericles carefully nursed his old car up through the gears as he drove home, he shook his head in wonder at the curveball that life had thrown at him that morning. He had worked very hard over the years at developing a tough emotional shell as far as women were concerned, and yet Kate had managed to cut through it like a hot knife through butter without even trying.

Part of him was worried what this meant, where tonight's dinner could lead him, but another, stronger part of him couldn't wait to find out and he started to whistle a tune as he pulled into the drive of his house and decided to call in to see his sister next door before going to work.

'Kalimera, Alexandra,' he called cheerfully as he walked through the front door and into the open plan lounge to find his sister sitting out on her balcony, staring out to sea as she did so often these days.

She jumped as he came into view. 'God, Pericles, you creep up like a cat trying to catch a mouse!'

'Sorry, Sister,' he said, bending down to kiss the top of her head 'I only wanted to see if there is anything you need before I go to work?'

'You asked me the same question before you went to do your son's work. Nothing has changed in the last two hours!'

He smiled at her, ignoring her sharpness. He knew she hated to feel like a burden. It pained him to see his sister this way; she had always been such a wild, carefree creature, but now, after losing her husband in a fishing accident and then suffering a stroke three years ago, she had become distant and understandably bitter, hating having to rely on him and her son for the simplest of tasks.

'How were things at the villa?' Alexandra asked him.

'Well, surprising is the answer to that,' he replied, pouring himself some water from the jug that he'd set out on the table for her that morning.

'I met the mother, her name is Kate, and we...' he stopped, trying to put into words what had happened between them.

'And you what?' she asked impatiently.

'We connected on some level; I don't know how to describe it. Something about her touched a part of me that I thought had shrivelled up and died decades ago.'

Alexandra looked at her brother in surprise. She had been the one to pick up the pieces when his wife had run off. Taking care of his son alongside her own and making sure they had food and a clean house every day. He had been a wreck for months, barely able to function. Then had come the incredible anger, which seemed to last for years, but that had at least fuelled him to get up and out of the house every day and start his life again.

Growing up, they had been very close. Her big brother had always looked out for her, protecting her from suiters until she had eventually found the one she wanted to marry. When her husband had managed to fatally blow himself up whilst illegally fishing, the bond between brother and sister had deepened, united in their abominable choice of partners, his being fickle and hers being unbelievably stupid.

When she had been taken ill, it had been natural for him to then look after her and he had built her a house next door to his own so she could have some independence. He had designed the house all on one level with everything easily accessible, even with her reduced mobility. So they had settled into a new routine where he popped in and out every day on some pretext or another, and she tried not to hate it too much.

But this news was out of the blue, the last thing she expected when he left the house this morning. She was aware he had had dalliances over the years, mostly with tourists, never with anybody who would expect anything but a quick fling, and she had truly believed he would grow old gracefully next door to her, neither of them needing anyone else but each other.

'So what does this mean? What can you possibly expect from this American woman except for heartache?' she asked harshly, looking at him searchingly and making him squirm in his chair.

'I don't know what this means. I have scarcely met her! We are going out for dinner tonight,' he smiled fondly at her. 'Wherever this should lead, you will always be the number one woman in my life, you know that.'

Alexandra felt instantly ashamed. He had, as usual, picked up on her feelings. Her first instinct had been to worry for herself, about how she would manage without his support and companionship, things which had never been threatened before. But looking at the light of excitement in his eyes, she knew that however, this meeting with the American woman went that evening, she would be a sorry excuse for a sister if she let her concerns stand in the way of his possible happiness.

'Well, go with my blessing, brother. If this woman does win your heart, she is infinitely fortunate and I will be happy to share you with her. It is time we had some fun in our lives.'

Linda had been awake for hours but she'd lain in bed, too scared to face the music. Eventually, her rumbling stomach insisted on her need for breakfast and the smell of warm croissants had driven her from under the blankets. She quickly washed and dressed before heading upstairs. As she walked into the kitchen, she found Kate, the last person she wanted to see, sat at the island drinking coffee and chatting with Maria. Kate was looking remarkably relaxed, she thought. In fact, she appeared to be positively buoyant.

'Good morning,' she said to alert them to her presence and stood hovering in the entrance, uncertain of her reception.

Kate turned around and beamed at her. 'Good morning, Linda, my love, come in and join us. Would you like coffee, a croissant?'

'Erm, both please,' Linda said, sliding onto a stool next to her, watching in astonishment as Kate rose and poured her a coffee and carefully arranged a croissant and a napkin on a plate before placing them in front of her.

'Forgive me Kate, but I thought you would hate me right now, yet here you are making me breakfast?'

Kate smiled at Linda's nervous face; she knew she had been too hard on this poor girl who had done nothing wrong, except fall in love with her son. She felt a pang of regret for the after-effects of Danial leaving her reaching so far into the future.

'Linda, it's you that needs to forgive me. I have been overbearing, controlling, and generally an all-round pain in the butt, and I really, really hope that we can move on from this.

Whatever happens between you and Scotty, and I will leave that for you both to decide. I hope that you and I will remain friends?'

Linda could not believe what she was hearing. Never would she have thought that this conversation would happen. She always imagined it was Scott's attitude that had to change, but hearing these words from his mother clicked something in her mind. She leant over and gave the older woman a heartfelt hug; 'I do hope we can be friends,' she said, and to her amazement, she meant every word.

Scott had spent the previous evening in Kassiopi. When he'd walked away from the painful scene at the beach, he hadn't a clue where he was going, he just knew he needed to get away, but when his wanderings brought him out onto the main road next to Nikos' supermarket, he knew he could easily walk down into the resort. He had gravitated into a busy bar called Illusions, the packed crowd and the loud music seeming the perfect antidote to his woes, and he was halfway through his first beer when a tap on his shoulder revealed Thomas the pool boy, who greeted him warmly and introduced him to his friends.

The rest of the evening passed in a blur as round after round was bought, and the camaraderie he felt helped distance himself from the trauma of the afternoon as he drank himself into oblivion. Luckily, his new friends had the sense to put him into a taxi in the early hours of the morning and he'd stumbled into the villa, bouncing off several walls before falling, fully clothed, onto his bed.

Marc bounced into his room a few hours later. 'Wakey, wakey, sleepyhead!' he shouted, pulling the curtains wide open and blinding him with sunlight that caused him to wince and roll over in his cocoon of sheets.

'God, keep your voice down,' he moaned, pulling a pillow over his head, which was throbbing alarmingly.

Marc considered the supine form of his friend for a moment before deciding he had to be cruel to be kind. 'Up and at 'em, fella. Today is another day and you are not going to spend it skulking down here. Let's go get some breakfast.' He ripped the sheet off Scott, giving him no choice but to comply.

When they finally came up for breakfast, they were amazed to find Kate and Linda chatting and laughing in such a carefree manner in the kitchen, the two women looking perfectly happy and relaxed in each other's company.

'Have we entered the Twilight Zone?' hissed Marc from the side of his mouth as they both pulled out stools to sit with the girls. Scott could only shrug his shoulders, his head hurting too much to shake it, and he grimaced at his friend, causing his sunburn to smart, lost for words.

He gratefully drank some of Maria's restorative coffee - she'd insisted on making him a cup of Greek coffee for some reason - and the thick liquid sweetened with lots of sugar was hitting the spot, making him feel a little more alert.

'Would you like breakfast?' the old woman asked, peering at him with her beady eyes. 'I do you eggs, bacon, yes?'

'Hell yes,' said Scott, thinking that food was a necessity at this point in the proceedings. He hadn't got round to eating yesterday, and he was feeling the effects.

'Could I have some too please, Maria my love' said Marc, smiling at the woman who turned scarlet but nodded her head curtly and happily got her frying pans out.

'Has anyone seen Charlotte this morning?' asked Linda, becoming aware that she hadn't seen or heard from her friend since yesterday.

Kate laughed, 'I have a feeling she is going to be too embarrassed to show her face this morning,' causing a look of panic to cross Marc's face. How could she possibly know?

But Kate continued and told them of her chat with Pericles that morning, well, the part with Charlotte messaging poor Thomas late last night, anyway. She didn't need to share the rest of that wonderful conversation; the conversation that had left her with a warm glow inside and a sense of anticipation for this evening. She felt a shudder of excitement run up her spine just thinking about it.

Marc wondered if he should share with them what had happened in the taxi last night. He felt bad that he'd been so brutal with Charlotte, but it had seemed like the only way to get through to the girl. He was thinking about sharing his reasoning for turning her down. Maybe now was the time, but before he could pluck up the courage, Peter walked in with his radiant smile and a hearty good morning to them all.

'Ok everyone, I'm glad to see that all is well with you?' he said with a slight question mark on the end, unsure of how to proceed after yesterday's drama and with his head pounding from last night's excesses. Emma was always such a bad influence on him, they'd ended up having far more beers than he had planned at the local beach bar and dancing the night away in the club-style atmosphere with a group of young Lithuanian's who seemed to have more vodka than sense.

It had been a great night, but he'd ended up sleeping on her sofa rather than driving home and had to drag himself up and out at the crack of dawn this morning, after about two hours sleep, to wiz home and feed his irate cats before coming in to work. He had splashed some cold water on his face, the icy liquid doing something to restore his senses, but he hadn't even had time to shave and was feeling pretty rough around the edges.

'Yes, everything is, surprisingly, absolutely fine,' Kate assured him, patting Linda's hand and smiling at her. Peter felt a little nonplussed but soldiered on, regardless.

'In that case, I thought I would see if there was anything anyone wanted to do today? We had scheduled a free day but if you want something organised let me know, or if anyone would care to go into Corfu town, I can take them and show them around.'

Scott pulled Linda's hand. 'Can I have a quick word?' he said, leading her into the lounge. 'Listen, I know it's too soon to talk about the big stuff, but I also know you had set your heart on us going to visit that abandoned village you were reading about. Together, alone,' he added for emphasis. 'What if we go and do that today and let's just enjoy the day together?'

Linda beamed at him; she didn't even have to think twice. 'I'd love to,' she said, nodding enthusiastically, and they walked back into the kitchen. She couldn't conceive that today would be so full of surprises. All of last night she had been dreading this morning and confronting everyone, but it seemed that her fears were unfounded.

'Peter, we want to go to the abandoned village that Linda read about in one of her guidebooks. Can you point us in the right direction?' Scott said, looking over at his mother and out of habit saying 'I hope that's ok, Ma?'

Kate stood up and smiled at them both. 'That is more than fine, I was planning to ask Peter to organise a massage and facial for me. I believe there's a company that comes to the villa?' this she directed at the concierge.

'Yes, of course,' he responded. 'Hold on, I will find their brochure' and he started rummaging through his bag.

'And while we are at it,' Kate announced, 'you kids may as well plan what you want to do tonight; ya'll have to root, hog, or die. I have been invited to dinner... by a man,' she added, a trifle defensively.

They all looked at her in amazement, not sure if she was joking or not, but it became evident from the look on her face that she was deadly serious. Linda and Scott looked at each other in amazement and Marc, slightly at a loss for what to say, went to make more coffee.

Peter slid the home spa brochure over to her and called to Marc, 'What about you? What are your plans for today? I guess you and Charlotte will be up to something?'

Marc looked at him steadily from next to the coffee machine.'I have no idea why you'd think that. I was thinking to take you up on the offer of a trip to town if that's possible?'

Peter's insides turned to jelly. The idea of spending a whole day with Marc was wonderful yet terrifying at the same time, but having made the offer and with everyone looking at him he realised he couldn't say no. Rubbing his hand self-consciously over his stubble and inwardly cursing Emma he said, 'of course, no problem. Why don't you get yourself ready while I show Scott and Linda where Old Perithia, the village they want to visit, is on the map and book in Kate's treatments.'

Peter got to work explaining all about the history of the old village to the couple and what to look out for when they were there, all the while his mind spinning with thoughts of Marc. 'There's a charming taverna down in the old square I can highly recommend,' he said once he was sure where they knew where they were going and that the GPS would take them on the right route.

He'd had some guests stuck halfway up the mountain on dirt tracks because the machine insisted on taking them the 'quickest' route rather than the sensible one. Next, he made the call and organised Kate's beauty treatments for her, explaining to the therapist on the phone exactly where the villa was and which treatments Kate required.

'So that's all booked for 3 pm for you. The therapist will arrive fifteen minutes or so before to set everything up. Will you need a taxi to go to dinner tonight?' he asked, wanting to make sure everything was in place before he went to town. He didn't want any unnecessary phone calls this afternoon.

'No,' she trilled girlishly, 'I am being picked up. In the meantime, I think I will spend some time next to the pool,' she added and, with that, she walked into her bedroom to get her swimming things.

Scott and Linda looked at each other in disbelief. They could never imagine Kate to act this way, but it seemed the Corfu atmosphere was getting under her skin and breathing new life into her. They got themselves ready and went out the front door; leaving Peter sat in the lounge waiting for Marc.

'He'll be awhile,' said Scott over his shoulder, 'he'll be doing his hair' and, laughing at his own witticism, he got into the car with Linda.

Peter took out his phone and started looking through the emails that had come in overnight. There was nothing urgent for him to do so, glancing round to make sure he was alone, he clicked on the Grindr icon. Up came the home screen with the map of his vicinity and the users available nearby. 'That can't be right' he thought, staring hard at the screen. 'There can't be a user with 30m of me here, we're in the middle of nowhere!' At that point, Marc jogged up the stairs, so he guiltily stuffed his phone into his pocket and stood up. Marc was looking as gorgeous as ever, wearing a blue, short-sleeved shirt that matched his eyes. Peter gulped; this was going to be quite a day.

In the kitchen, Maria, who was clearing up after breakfast, looked furtively around, then picked up Scott's coffee cup, turning it clockwise three times and peering into the dregs. After a moment, considering what she saw there, a huge smile split her raisin-like face and, humming, she continued with her work.

In her room, Charlotte was indeed too embarrassed to go upstairs. She had woken with a splitting headache hours ago, so had taken a couple of painkillers and washed them down with tap water from the bathroom rather than go upstairs and face everyone. As she looked at her reflection in the mirror, she was horrified. 'God, my eyes look like two fried eggs in a slop bucket,' she muttered to herself and used some wipes to remove the makeup smeared across her face.

She had no recollection of the end of last night, but her faithful phone revealed her antics soon enough. 'Oh my God' she thought to herself 'what on earth made me text the pool boy?' She curled up back in bed, pulling the blanket around her for comfort, trying to put together the pieces of last night, but all she had was fragments. She vaguely remembered a taxi and there was a flash of Marc's face in closeup, looking concerned, but that was it.

She heard the sound of voices and then the front door closing and engines starting then becoming distant before silence descended on the villa. She crept out of bed and went slowly upstairs and was very surprised to find Maria still busy in the kitchen.

'Good morning, Miss Charlotte,' said the maid, placing a cup of coffee in front of her. 'I wait for you, I think today you will be needing cooked breakfast, yes?' To her surprise, Charlotte found that she was hungry. In fact, she could murder some bacon and eggs. She nodded and smiled gratefully at Maria before taking her cup outside to sit and look at the view.

A short while later, the woman put a plate in front of her along with a glass of freshly squeezed juice. 'Eat. Drink. You will feel better,' she said sternly, picking up the empty cup and glancing in it.

'Thank you, Maria. I'm sure this will help, but it will take more than breakfast to make me feel better,' said Charlotte, disconsolately picking up her knife and fork.

'Every heart sings a song, incomplete until another heart whispers back. Those who wish to sing always find a song. You will find love where you least expect it, child.'

And with that, the maid turned and walked back into the villa, leaving Charlotte open-mouthed in shock.

Scott and Linda had found the village of Old Perithia, relishing the drive that took them up the mountain and had spent a magical hour wandering around the old buildings taking lots of photographs before stopping at the taverna in the square that Peter had mentioned for some coffee and an amazing walnut cake.

They still hadn't spoken about yesterday, instead opting to enjoy their surroundings and each other's company. The views on the drive up here had been spectacular. Situated almost at the top of the highest mountain on Corfu, the village was nestled in a safe place, away from the coast and marauders of old.

'It's hard to imagine living up here, so far away from everything,' Linda said, scooping up the last of the cake with her spoon. 'That was delicious. I don't think I will eat again all day, I am stuffed.' she added.

'That's a shame. I was thinking that tonight we could go to dinner together. Peter mentioned this first-class place in Kassiopi, it's only up the road' said Scott, looking hopefully at her. Linda was unsure of what to say. She had enjoyed this time with him and she had appreciated the fact he hadn't broached the subject about *them*, although she was sure he was desperate to. Then she thought of Kate and how different she had been this morning, holding out an olive branch and going on a date. 'To hell with it, why not' she said to him, smiling at the look of delight on his face and hoping she wouldn't regret her decision.

Marc didn't know why he'd suggested going to town with the concierge; he only knew he didn't want to be in the villa when Charlotte woke up. Strangely, it wasn't as awkward as he'd feared on the hour-long drive down the coast road, Peter chatted away easily, pointing out landmarks, even stopping at one of the lookout points shortly before a bay called Kalami so Marc could take some panoramic shots of the stunning views.

'Kalami Bay is where they filmed part of the James Bond film 'For your eyes only', and of course was home to Lawrence Durrell, the writer for a while.' Peter told him as he angled his camera to capture the best shot. 'The house where he lived is a taverna now. You would have seen it when you were out on the boat, maybe you should go for dinner there one night.'

'I'm not sure how things are going to pan out now,' Marc mused. 'Everything's a bit up in the air, even though Scott and Linda seemed fine with each other this morning.'

'Don't forget you have the trip to the vineyard planned for tomorrow,' said Peter, as they walked back to the car to continue their journey. 'Even the family from the hotel are going and it really is a fantastic day out. It's a remarkable place, I'm sure you'll appreciate it.'

'That's true,' Marc conceded. 'We will have to see how the land lies when we get back from town, see who out of the group still wants to go. Hopefully, they're still up for it, it sounds great,' he said, smiling at Peter, causing butterflies to erupt in his stomach.

As they got closer to town and the road started to get busier, Marc admired the way Peter easily manoeuvred through the erratic traffic, taking each traffic offence that occurred around them without batting an eyelid, until they found a parking spot.

'So, Corfu had been ruled by Venice, France and Britain,' said Peter as they began to walk into the town 'but unusually for Greece, never by the Turks. That's what makes this island so unique; the strong Italian influence is even reflected in the dialect. This way,' he added, leading them through an archway into the old town.

Marc loved Corfu town, the beautiful facades of bygone eras, cobbled streets crammed with shops selling everything from olive oil soap to fur coats, which he found bizarre in this heat. They made their way to St. Spiridion church, the ornately ceilinged final resting place of the patron saint of the island; although Peter informed him, they dusted him off and paraded the coffin around on special occasions.

Wandering up to the Liston area, they heard the sound of a philharmonic band practising high up in one of the many splendid Venetian buildings that lined the streets, adding to the atmosphere and making Marc feel as if he was on a film set.

‘Let’s go and grab a coffee,’ said Peter, looking at Marc for assent.

‘In this heat? I would have thought something cold would be in order’ he smiled back.

'Ah, I am going to introduce you to the fantastic cold coffees we have here' and, laughing at the look of distaste on Marc's face added 'I insist you try it, I know it sounds weird but believe me, it works.'

‘Well, as you’re being so masterful, I guess I have no choice but to do as I’m told,’ said Marc, walking on, leaving Peter looking after him. He was definitely getting mixed signals with this guy. Trotting to catch up with him, they reached the famous Liston, which was teeming with tourists, obviously on guided tours, following the raised baton of their guides like school children.

They chose a café, Peter ordered their coffees, and they fell into a companionable silence for a while. ‘So yesterday didn’t quite go to plan’ said Peter, taking a sip from his Freddo cappuccino once it arrived and smiling at Marc, who chuckled.

‘No, not for anyone I’m thinking,’ he responded, adding ‘this coffee is amazing, you were right.’

Peter wasn’t sure what to make of his statement, but felt the need to probe.

‘So you and Charlotte?’ he said, whilst feigning deep interest in the cricket match that was taking place on the green in front of where they were sat.

‘Charlotte and I will never be an item,’ Marc said with equal attention to the action on the field, taking another sip before continuing hesitatingly.

'I...' he paused; 'I'm not interested in girls, despite what you may have heard.'

Peter's heart was racing, pounding in his chest as he absorbed what this man was telling him. Was he saying what he thought he was saying?

He wasn't quite sure how to respond and sat quietly for a while, trying to formulate his next sentence.

'So you mean...' he trailed off, not sure if he dare say it.

'Yes. I mean, I'm gay,' said Marc quietly.

'So you've never told your friends that you're gay?' he asked hesitantly, not sure if it was his place to continue this conversation. Marc silently shook his head, staring into the middle distance. 'I have never told anybody,' he admitted. 'To be honest, I'm not sure why I am telling you,' he added, looking directly at Peter for the first time.

Peter held his gaze. 'That would explain why there was someone close by on Grindr at the villa.' He smiled, causing a brief look of panic, and then sudden understanding, to cross Marc's face.

'Oh my God, I hadn't even thought to turn off my location; I didn't imagine anyone would be looking at that app over here!'

'Well, your secret is safe with me. I have to say, your life would be simpler if you came out, but that's something you have to do in your own time. I know it's not easy,' said Peter. Then, taking a deep breath, he added, 'the only reason I mention it is because I find you very attractive, and this is the first time in a long time that this has happened to me. And one thing I have learnt is that you should take a chance when these things happen because they don't happen very often.'

Marc was astonished. He'd been aware that they had clicked, but he was so used to hiding his sexuality that he hadn't let it register fully. He hadn't allowed himself to admit that he was drawn to this lovely man.

Coming from a deeply religious Texan family whose cattle rich patriarch was so macho, he exuded testosterone and Marc had never felt he could tell people how he felt. His father would disown him for sure if he ever got a whiff of it, which was why he'd worked very hard at cultivating his playboy image. His four brothers had opted to stay on and settle at the family ranch, marrying early and producing a never-ending stream of nieces and nephews, and were constantly ribbing him about when he was going to settle down.

There had been times when he'd thought of telling Scott. He knew his friend would be accepting and supportive, but felt it was a huge secret to ask someone to keep for you and Scott would struggle with being duplicitous. He didn't want to lay that particular burden at his door; he had enough to deal with in his own life.

'I can't believe I've told you this,' he said grinning, 'there must be something in the air!'

'Corfu tends to have that effect on people' Peter grinned back at him. 'I am going to go out on a limb here,' he said, taking a deep breath and wondering at his own bravery, 'Would you care to have dinner with me tonight?' He sat back in his chair, terrified that he might have ruined something special that was forming between them. He needn't have worried. Marc didn't hesitate.

'I can honestly say I would like that very much' he said, and at a shout from the cricket pitch, they both returned their gaze to the game, smiling to themselves, marvelling at the turn of events and shyly glancing at each other as they drank their coffees.

Charlotte had finished her wonderful, much-needed breakfast and was indeed feeling better as she drank her second cup of coffee when Kate wandered up from the pool. The older woman smiled at her and, placing her water carefully on the glass tabletop, sat down opposite her.

'I gather you had an interesting evening... or not, as the case may be,' she said, looking attentively at Charlotte's face to gauge her reaction.

Charlotte flushed a deep red and covered her face with her hands. 'Oh god, I guess you know about me texting Thomas' she exclaimed. 'How did you find out? Did he tell everybody when he came in this morning?'

'Actually, it was his father who came by this morning; the poor boy was too scared to set foot in the villa,' answered Kate, taking a sip of water and looking at the girl with kind eyes. 'Although I am not sure what frame of mind you were in when you sent that message, I am going to say thank you.'

Charlotte glanced up, brow furrowed, looking confused. 'What are you thanking me for? I thought you would be furious with me.'

'Well,' said Kate, 'if you hadn't sent that message last night, his father would not have come here and I wouldn't have met the loveliest man I have had the pleasure of talking with in a long time.'

Charlotte looked thoughtfully at Kate. She could see a subtle difference in her. She looked softer somehow, and there was an undeniable glow about her.

'You mean to tell me that you've hit it off with the hottie's dad?' she said in disbelief.

'I rather think I did. As it happens, we are going out for dinner tonight,' Kate replied, sounding amazed. 'And if I was you, I would go down to the harbour bar tonight where Thomas and his friends like to hang out and try to have a conversation with the poor lad rather than ambushing him by text. Unless, of course, you still have designs on Marc?'

'You don't miss much, do you, Kate?' Charlotte smiled at her. 'But no, I think I shall have to give up on Marc once and for all. He doesn't seem interested in me despite my best efforts. Sometimes I wish I were a little kid again, skinned knees are easier to fix than broken hearts.'

'All the more reason for you to go out tonight. Put your glad rags on and go and enjoy yourself, girl. I've realised that life is too short to be hung up on a particular man, especially one that doesn't want you,' she said, thinking about the years she'd wasted hung up on Danial.

'You're probably right. I might see if Linda fancies going out. I'm not sure I'd have the guts to go there on my own. In the meantime, I think I'm going to walk down to the beach and take a dip in the sea. The water looked amazing yesterday and I am dying to jump in, it might help clear my head.' She stood and gathered her things. 'By the way, where is everybody this morning? It's very quiet.'

'Well, I am glad to say Scott and Linda have gone out together to explore some boring old village in the mountains and Peter has taken pity on Marc and taken him into Corfu Town for the day, so hopefully they are all enjoying themselves.'

Scott and Linda were indeed enjoying themselves, even though the hire car had broken down on the way back down the mountain. It had stuttered to a halt just as they entered the village at the bottom of the winding mountain road and refused to start again. Digging the rental agreement out of the glovebox, Scott found and called the number for the car hire company. When he managed to get through and make himself understood, he had to send Linda running into the nearby shop to ask which village they were in so he could explain to the Zeus staff exactly where they were.

'Well, it appears we're going to be here a while. Apparently, it's siesta time,' he said in disbelief, putting his phone on the dash while he stuffed the paperwork back into the glovebox, jabbing it angrily to make it fit. He had been so determined that today should be perfect and now it was all going wrong. Linda was not going to be impressed with him after this turn of events.

'Not to worry,' said Linda, smiling brightly at him. 'It's all part of the adventure. Look, there's a bar over there, let's go and have a drink.'

Grateful for her optimistic frame of mind, he nodded happily, and they made their way over the road to the bar. As they walked in, they were greeted by a wall of sound and the dying strains of 'happy birthday' being sung very badly and raucous laughter.

'Looks like someone's having a good time' she smiled as they walked up to the bar, indicating the group sitting at a large table littered with empty glasses and bottles.

Once they'd ordered their drinks, the barman, a giant of a young man, told them that their first drinks were on the birthday boy. 'He's buying drinks for everyone today,' he chuckled. 'I think he's going to wake up a poor man tomorrow!'

'Wow, that's very kind' said Scott. 'Which one is he?'

'The gentleman at the end in the bright blue jumper' said the barman, pointing. 'His name is Dave.'

Scott and Linda walked over, drinks in hand. 'Sorry to interrupt. We wanted to say thanks for the drinks and happy birthday,' he said, holding his beer aloft.

'Yes, many happy returns,' Linda added, smiling at the group around the table.

'No problem, mate,' said Dave in a very British accent. 'Why don't you join us, reprobates? You might bring a little decorum to the table,' and, laughing, he stood up and shook Scott's hand. 'I'm Dave, as you've probably gathered; let me introduce you to the gang.'

Soon extra chairs were pulled up, and the conversation was flowing as quickly as the drinks and, before she knew it, Linda realised it was late afternoon. Not only that, she and Scott had not stopped laughing and chatting the entire time and not once had he looked at his phone to check for messages from his mother.

'You do realise it seems as if we are stranded here?' she said, leaning in so he could hear her. 'There's no sign of that mechanic and it's nearly evening time,' she grinned.

'I feel like we're playing hooky' he grinned back at her. 'Actually, wait there, I have an idea' and with that, he leapt up and strode over to the bar. She watched him go in amazement. It was hard to believe that yesterday he'd asked her to marry him and she'd said no, yet here they were enjoying each other's company as if nothing had happened. If anything, they seemed to be getting on better than ever. It was quite bizarre.

When he returned a few minutes later, his grin was even wider. 'Right, Linda, I have at long last taken your advice and planned something by myself. I have booked us a room, together I might add, in that small apartment block right over there.' He pointed across the street to a charming looking old building with faded green shutters and purple bougainvillaea draped unrestrainedly across its façade.

Linda looked into his eyes for a long, hard minute. It seemed too soon. After the drama of yesterday, she had never in her wildest dreams thought that 24 hours later they would be sat here, without his mum, discussing spending the night together. She couldn't help but smile as she saw the flicker of doubt in his bravado flash across his face and he bit his lip, worry contorting his face.

'Scott, I would love to spend the night with you,' she murmured, and leaned back in, this time to give him a long, tender kiss. They were interrupted by a loud cheer from the all but forgotten crowd they were sitting with and another round of drinks was ordered.

Meanwhile, Peter and Marc had finished their coffees and were wandering down the narrow alleys as dusk fell, to where the car was parked by the Old Port, stopping to admire shop windows and churches along the way.

'This is such a beautiful town,' Marc said. 'I didn't realise there was so much history here, it's quite remarkable.'

'It's one of the reasons I came here,' replied Peter. 'That and a bit of a wake-up call with work many years ago which made me realise life is too short to be stuck in a rut.'

Marc took on board his words, trying to imagine a time when he could catapult himself out of his particular rut. It didn't seem possible; his fears of what would happen in his life if he came out were so deep-seated his brain wouldn't allow him to consider it. It terrified him to think of even contemplating having that particular conversation with his father. He could only imagine his reaction to finding out his youngest son was gay. There would be carnage. He shivered at the thought and brought his mind back into the present, an altogether more pleasant state of affairs.

'There doesn't seem much point going back to the villa,' Marc said, smiling at him as they got into the car. 'Shall we go straight out for something to eat?'

'Sure,' Peter responded. 'Let's drive back up the coast and go to a little place I know near Kalami.'

'Sounds perfect,' Marc responded, as he put on the seat belt. 'I'm completely in your hands, Petey.' Peter flushed, for the first time in his life finding the diminutive use of his name musical, and smiled to himself as he started the car, flicked on the lights and reversed out of the parking space.

Charlotte had spent a fantastic afternoon on Avlaki beach, the restorative powers of the sun and sea working their magic on her body and mind and helping put yesterday's embarrassments into perspective. The water was as amazing as it had looked and she alternated between swimming widths of the bay with slow and steady strokes and lying on the sunbed enjoying the heat from the sun whilst watching the children's surf lessons going on a short distance away.

By late afternoon, she felt fully recovered from the excesses of the day before and was starting to feel hungry again. She decided to amble back to the restaurant where the 'non' party had happened yesterday to grab something to eat. She collected her things together and started to make her way down the stony beach towards the restaurant. As she neared the windsurf school, she saw the instructor pulling in the last of his vessels from the sea and couldn't help but admire his strong, tanned back. 'Well, that's a fine-looking man' she thought to herself appreciatively, so she pulled up short, startled when he turned and she realised that it was Manolis, from the boat trip.

He looked up and saw her, and his face broke into a smile. 'Miss Charlotte' he called, 'how are you today?'

'A little out of sorts,' she replied, walking towards him, hoisting her bag more snugly onto her shoulder 'and so hungry my belly thinks my throat's been cut.'

He looked at her for a second then said 'the one word I understood there was hungry, are you going to the taverna?'

'I am, yes,' she replied. 'Sorry, we southerners are hard to understand sometimes. What are you doing here; I thought you worked on the boat?'

'Like most people here, I work two jobs,' he said. 'We have only a few months in the summer to make all our wages so I do this as well.'

He slung a couple of boards easily over his shoulder. 'Come on, I need to take these back,' he said, nodding in the direction of the restaurant. Charlotte noticed a sign next to it advertising the windsurf centre.

'It must be great to teach the kids windsurfing; I teach swimming back home to under 12's and it's fantastic. I love to see the look on their faces when they finally get it, it's so rewarding. I can't imagine many jobs where you get the same sense of achievement.'

He nodded enthusiastically 'I much prefer my work teaching. I love helping the kids learn to do this,' Manolis said. 'The extra money from the boat is great, but it is not so rewarding.'

'It was pretty entertaining when we were on there, though!' Charlotte teased as they stopped outside the restaurant. On impulse she added 'what are you doing now, would you like to join me for something to eat?'

'That would be great. My belly also thinks that something has been cut,' he teased back. 'I will have to finish putting the equipment away then I will be there.'

At the villa, Kate was trying to relax in the hands of the masseuse but was finding it difficult to block out the image of Pericles smiling at her over his coffee cup that morning. As the masseuse's hand rubbed tension from her back and neck, she tried to distract herself by deciding what to wear that night. It had been so many years since she had been on a date; she for once, was at a loss for an outfit. She didn't want to be overdressed as she assumed they would be going somewhere simple to eat, so she was running through her wardrobe trying to visualise the best combination.

As she sat, after the massage, to let her face pack set, she decided on a plain full-length skirt and blouse ensemble she knew she would be comfortable in and poured herself a large glass of Whispering Angel for Dutch courage, lounging on the terrace whilst the mask worked its magic.

As the treatment tightened on her face, she sat gazing out to sea, marvelling at today's developments. Could she really be going out with another man? After Danial had left her, she had sworn to never let anyone else into her life and it had not been an issue. No one else had managed to breach the wall of steel she had shuttered her emotions away with, up until now.

While she was showering, she considered cancelling. What was the point, after all? But she realised she had no way of contacting him other than through Thomas, and she certainly didn't want to startle that poor boy even further. So she towelled herself off and proceeded to get dressed, picking up the clothes she'd carefully laid out on the bed earlier.

At exactly 8 pm that night, she stood fidgeting and patting her hair, waiting by the front door, butterflies fluttering around in her stomach, making her feel sure she was not going to be able to eat a single thing at dinner. She was looking at her phone for the hundredth time to check when she felt, rather than heard, a resounding noise and a huge, growling motorbike came thundering down the drive and skidded to a stop in front of her. She looked aghast at the machine and then up into the laughing face of Pericles.

'You should see your face!' he howled, slapping his thigh 'I guess you are not used to motorbikes.'

'I most certainly am not! You cannot seriously expect me to get on the back of that thing,' she snapped, her shock at his arrival making her forget her nerves. Although she had to admit the old Triumph Bonneville seemed to suit his personality somehow: old but strong with an edge of something she couldn't quite put her finger on.

Pericles kicked the stand into place easily, swung his leg over the bike, and walked over to her. Taking her hands in his, he looked deep into her eyes and said, 'If you are that uncomfortable with the idea, then I will go and bring my car. But Kate, you and I have spent too long, I think, being careful. Not trying anything new and so not having any fun. I believe tonight is the time for us to both let loose a little, don't you?'

As she gazed into his velvet brown eyes, a bubble of something welled up inside her; the nervous butterflies had been replaced with excitement.

'Give me a minute,' she said and ran back into the villa. A few minutes later, she reappeared wearing a different outfit. This time she had on Capri pants, much more suited for a pillion ride. He smiled at her obvious consent and, having climbed back on to his bike, held out his hand to help her jump on behind him. He reached behind him to take her hands yet again, this time pulling them around his waist.

'Hold on tight,' he said over his shoulder 'I wouldn't want to lose you now.' And she clasped his waist as a shiver ran through her, excitement and nerves battling for dominance.

Clutching on to him for dear life as he made his way back up the drive and along the bumpy track to the main road, she was surprised when he did pick up speed to find herself laughing with exhilaration as they sped up the road, flying around the bends with ease.

The ride that night was a revelation to Kate. With the warm air blowing through her hair, the vibration of the uneven roads reverberating through her and everything passing by in a blur, she felt liberated. For the first time in her life, she felt completely free and unfettered, and it was a wonderful sensation.

When he eventually slowed down and turned off the main road onto an incredibly steep drive leading down to a beach, gravity pulling her even closer to his warmth, she was almost disappointed that the journey was over. She looked up at the restaurant they had pulled in next to, which looked dark, apart from a dim light near the back, and decidedly closed. The tiered veranda at the front of the building was large enough to accommodate a host of tables, but they were all bare, giving off a lonely, abandoned air.

'Are you sure we're in the right place?' she asked him, looking around uncertainly. Smiling with an impish look on his face he took her by the hand and led her down some wooden steps onto the sandy beach below and there, a little before the shoreline, was a table set for two, surrounded by flickering candles casting a romantic glow over the scene.

'Oh, my,' she whispered as she took it all in. 'I feel just like Shirley Valentine.'

Pericles pulled out a chair for her and snapped his fingers, causing a waiter to miraculously appear by their side, bearing three carafes of wine balanced carefully on a tray.

'I didn't know what you prefer, so I have ordered red, white and rose' he said, looking at her earnestly. Kate chose the rose whilst he went for the red and, after pouring their drinks, the waiter gave them menus and discreetly disappeared.

'I don't understand,' said Kate, 'this place looks closed, yet here we are.'

'It is closed,' Pericles smiled. 'I have arranged it especially for us.'

Kate was taken aback; this seemed far too grand a gesture from someone she had just met, someone down at heel who certainly couldn't afford grand gestures. She was just trying to think how to tactfully suggest they go fifty-fifty when, seeing the concern on her face, her eyes having taken in his simple clothes and making assumptions, he decided to put her out of her misery.

Throwing his menu to one side, Pericles said 'you see all this?' He stood up and gestured to the dark building behind them and the expanse of land beyond where she could see a cluster of villas perched on the hill, their lights twinkling in the distance. 'It's mine,' he stated simply.

'What, all of it?' Kate asked, shocked.

'Yes Madam Kate, all of it. So if I decide to close my restaurant for a night because I have one special guest, then I will. Now, stop staring, close your mouth and let's order some food!'

Kates's head was spinning, trying to take everything in, which is why, for the first time in many years, she did what she was told, and started looking at the menu. She made a few tentative suggestions but gave way to his judgement for the rest of the choices. After all, it was his place. He was sure to know what was best.

Soon the table was overflowing as dish after dish kept appearing. It felt as if he was trying to woo her with food and, in the end, laughing, she had to tell the waiter to stop.

'I can't possibly eat another thing,' she said, rubbing her stomach for emphasis and pushing her plate to one side.

'I'm sure you can manage some more wine,' he said, indicating her empty glass. 'You seem to be enjoying the rose?'

'It's wonderful,' she responded, proffering her glass to the waiter who had yet again reappeared with another carafe. 'I love fine wines. Where does this come from? Is it French?'

'Like everything you've tasted tonight, it's Corfiot,' he said proudly. 'Those grapes come from the land around my house and my sister and I press them ourselves every September..... Well, now she can only watch, but she's always there to enjoy the process. My family have worked this land for centuries. We were good old-fashioned peasant stock living down by the sea when the rich all hid up in the mountain villages, laughing every time we were plundered,' he took a long sip of his wine. 'Now we can laugh back, tourism has made all us seashore land-owning peasants rich!'

Kate was impressed despite herself; it was hard to imagine his family struggling to work the land, which surely must have been less fertile down by the sea, and survive the marauding pirates. She felt a sense of history to this place, to this man, which she hadn't come across before, and it intrigued her. It was part of what was drawing her to him. As hard as she tried to ignore it, there was a magnetism there that she was helpless to resist, and she could feel herself falling for him with every minute that went by.

Charlotte had been unable to find a free table at the restaurant, which was full to bursting, so when Manolis joined her a few minutes later, she was still standing uncertainly at the entrance.

'Too busy, huh?' he said, smiling at her.

'It certainly seems popular; I guess we could wait for a table to come free.'

'That will take too long for a damsel dying of starvation,' he laughed 'I tell you what, let's go to Kassiopi, there's a fast food place there that does the best gyros in town, and they do it quickly!'

She eagerly agreed, and they rode in his car, chatting companionably on the short drive. He drove down to the harbour front, carefully avoiding the mindless tourists wandering in the road, and managed to squeeze his car into the one small gap available before they walked back up the cobbled road to the main square and the No. 7 grill room, renowned for its local food.

They claimed a table in the corner and, over the buzz of the conversation around them, they ordered their food from the waiter who took their order and quickly returned with the cans of Coke Light they'd asked for and two large gyros.

'I love this village,' said Charlotte, trying to catch the tzatziki that was dribbling down her chin. 'Our concierge brought us here the other day; it has such a friendly atmosphere.'

'I'm glad you like it, it's my home village,' Manolis responded, smiling 'How's your gyros?'

'It's as good as all get out,' she said emphatically, taking another large bite and causing a spurt of the spicy tomato sauce to shoot down her white t-shirt. 'I always seem to end up covered in food when you're around,' she said, laughing as she dabbed at it ineffectually with her napkin before deciding to go to the bathroom to try and rinse out the worst of it.

Looking at her reflection in the mirror as she ran her top under the tap, she realised what a state she looked. Her sea-washed hair was all over the place and tangled, her unmade face glowing from her time in the sun and, of course, remnants of gyros on her face. She couldn't believe she was out in public looking this way, and she also couldn't believe she had been so carefree with her appearance in front of a man.

Thinking about it, she hadn't even given it a thought, and it dawned on her that for the first time in her life, she was in the company of a man she felt completely comfortable with. As she walked back to the table, she reassessed Manolis, who was chatting and laughing with the owner of the restaurant, who, it appeared, was an old friend.

She took in again his strong shoulders, his tight-fitting green t-shirt emphasising his form and highlighting his eyes, which she hadn't realised were a gorgeous hazel colour, flecked with green and gold and surrounded by long dark lashes. His sensuous mouth was permanently turned up and smiling, his sense of humour and kindness shining through with every move he made.

'How on earth did I miss this?' she thought to herself as she sat back down at the table, still staring at him but with new, appreciative eyes now.

'What?' Manolis said self-consciously 'have I got food on my face?' he grabbed a handful of napkins and started wiping his mouth.

She laughed at his little boy lost face and said, 'No honey, you're just fine. Absolutely damn fine.'

Scott and Linda had at last taken their leave of the friendly crowd in the village bar and walked a little uncertainly over the road to the apartment building, leaning on each other for support and giggling like kids. As they reached the arched doorway, Scott stopped in his tracks and turned towards Linda, becoming serious.

'I know you didn't agree to marry me but I still want to carry you over the threshold.' He hiccupped at this point, spoiling the effect, and they both dissolved in fits of giggles again.

He opened the door and, gathering his breath, he swept her up in his arms and tried to walk through the doorway, misjudging the narrow opening and banging her head with a thud on the way through.

'Oh my God, I'm so sorry,' he said, gently putting her down.

She laughed, rubbing the spot that had made contact with the door frame 'Don't worry Scott, I'll live' she replied, and she took him by the hand and led him up the stairs to room number 1 where, as promised, the key was there in the lock for them.

Just before they entered the room, he took her in his arms and whispered, 'are you sure about this, Linda?'

Smiling up at his handsome face, she answered him with a kiss, and then another, their passion swiftly increasing, reaching a level they hadn't experienced before. They started to frantically pull at each other's clothes. Scrabbling at the key in the door behind him, Scott eventually managed to turn it without his lips leaving hers and they fell through the door and onto the large double bed, waiting for them.

It seemed to Linda like a completely new experience making love to Scott that night, something new found yet familiar, something old yet exciting. Their recent differences added another level to every kiss and every touch, building to a frenzy until finally when he entered her, she cried out his name with such passion he came immediately.

As they lay, panting and spent, in the moments after, he apologised sheepishly. He'd never had a problem holding out before. A mental rundown of his monthly targets usually put paid to that, but this time, his bonus hadn't even entered his head. As they lay there, still entwined, enjoying the afterglow, he was surprised to find himself becoming aroused again, and he started to kiss her shoulder, then her neck, making his way to her mouth before working back down to her hardening nipples, causing her to moan his name once more, much more softly this time, encouraging him to explore her body further until she came with an extended scream that must have woken the whole village. He fell exhausted by her side, smiling with the pleasure he'd given her.

Peter had taken Marc to one of his favourite restaurants, Dimitris, overlooking Kalami Bay. Unprepossessing from the outside, Marc was blown away as they were led out onto the vine-covered terrace to see the view that was revealed.

'Wow,' he exclaimed, smiling disarmingly at the waitress. 'If the food is as good as the view I'm in for a fantastic meal.' She flushed a little and seated them at the table in the corner, offering the best vantage point to enjoy the scenery. The Albanian mountains in the distance glowing in the final rays of the sun and looking like an Impressionist painting.

They chatted over carafes of smooth tasting house wine while the staff efficiently ran back and forth bringing plates of delicious foods. Toasted pitas and a selection of delectable local dips were swiftly followed by plates filled with large, aromatic garlicky shrimps, perfectly grilled pork souvlaki and fresh-tasting salads bursting with flavour and the boys demolished the lot, savouring every mouthful.

As they were finishing up, still picking at morsels from the plates despite being incredibly full, a blood-red full moon made its gentle appearance over the mountains, the glow from it casting a magical light over the sea.

Smiling at him while the plates were being cleared away, Peter said, 'You will have to save room for dessert; they have the most amazing brownies here that you have to try.'

'You could have told me that half an hour ago,' laughed Marc. 'I'm not sure I can manage a whole one. I tell you what, why don't we share?'

Peter, feeling a little self-conscious, ordered the dessert to share. He couldn't believe today's turn of events. It was not how he had expected his day to pan out and, as he looked at the gorgeous man sitting opposite him, he realised with a start he hadn't given work thought for hours. That hadn't happened in such a long time.

'You do realise you have achieved the impossible and distracted me from my work?' he told Marc as the brownie was placed on the table between them with two spoons. Marc picked up a spoon to pass to him and, as their fingers brushed together, a bolt of electricity shot through Pete's body, causing him to flush the same colour as the moon.

'I am very glad to hear it; I would hate to think you had your mind on anything but me at this point.'

With brownies being the last thing on his mind, Peter made a big show of taking a big spoonful of the delicious dessert, all the while pictures of where this night might lead running through his mind. Was it possible he'd finally met the one? They seemed perfectly in tune with each other. They hadn't stopped talking and laughing all day, and he certainly found him attractive. He was sure that Marc felt the same way judging by the looks he was giving him, and he liked cats too, which was a bonus. Happily finishing off the dessert, he wished there was a way of retaining this magical feeling forever.

Kate's mind was currently in a whirl. She was in the arms of a charming, funny, good looking man, dancing on a moonlit beach on Corfu and had never felt so alive in her life. The incredible full moons' unusual red tint was bathing the beach in a warm glow which reflected her feelings exactly, especially when he kissed her so tenderly.

'Tell me, did you organise this wonderful moonlight along with everything else?' she asked playfully.

'That I can't take credit for,' he said, smiling down at her. 'The Gods are without doubt smiling on us as they do when Eros plays his games and wins.'

As the song came to an end, he pulled away from her and led her back to the table. She was shocked at how her body missed his warmth. When they were seated, he looked at her intently.

'So, Miss Kate, where do we go from here?'

'I... I don't know. We just have another two days on Corfu,' she replied sorrowfully. 'I'm not sure where that leaves us.' She felt as if a bucket of icy water had been thrown over her, even thinking about leaving him. The warm glow from moments before rapidly leaving her body causing her to pull her cardigan tighter around herself.

'Well, I think we need to explore this further. I am not prepared to let you disappear out of my life. I have lived so long without romance I had forgotten how wonderful it can feel.'

Kate's emotions were in turmoil. She felt the same way as him, but she lived over 6,000 miles away. How could they possibly make this work? Could she possibly come and live here to be with this man? Her heart sang yes, but her mind trotted out a million reasons why she could not. Frustration making tears well up in her eyes. She said, 'I have to go home, Pericles. My life is there, my son. Maybe you could come to Houston?' she asked, already knowing the answer but trying, anyway.

'I too am deeply rooted here with my family and businesses. I guess in the winter months I could possibly travel...' he paused 'but I don't believe either of us will be satisfied with a long-distance relationship. It would never be enough for either of us. I think it would just extend the agony of eventually being apart.'

They sat in despairing silence for a few minutes, both of them cursing Eros and his machinations, bringing them together now, here, when it was impossible for them to be together. It seemed cruelly ironic after their years of being successfully and happily independent to be brought so swiftly down to earth by one fortuitous meeting.

Eventually, he stood up and came around the table. He crouched down in front of her and gently lifted her chin, smiling up at her. 'Don't look so sad. We still have two days. Let's make the most of what time we have and savour every minute. We can show our children how to love!' he said laughingly, and he reached up to kiss her through her tears.

Charlotte and Manolis had walked back down to the harbour after their late lunch and stood chatting whilst watching the tour boats offload rowdy groups who'd spent the day on the famous local 'Booze Cruises', laughing at the tourist's efforts to walk in a straight line as they came down the gangplank, holding onto the guide ropes for dear life.

'So, what are your plans now?' he asked as he checked the time on his phone.

'I'm not sure,' she said, looking around as if for inspiration and smiling uncertainly at him. 'Everyone else seemed to have plans for today and to be honest, I'd be just as happy keeping a low profile as you can imagine.'

Manolis laughed. She had found herself telling him all about last night and her embarrassment this morning at her drunken antics. He had been remarkably cool about the whole thing and seemed to find the entire story hilarious, especially as the Thomas in question was his cousin, and he could well imagine the poor boy's horror at being 'sexted'.

'Well, if you want, we could have a little adventure that doesn't require anyone else,' he said. 'I just have to go home and check on something, then I could come back and meet you at Bataria beach, just around the headland there' and he pointed to a narrow road running up the side of the harbour. She nodded her assent, and he explained exactly where he would meet her once he had done what he needed to do.

'You can have another swim. The water there is beautiful. I will be as quick as I can.'

With that, he set off towards his car and Charlotte, after admiring his retreat, followed his instructions and made her way around the headland until she came to the bay he had told her about. The water was indeed beautiful. This island seemed to be non-stop picture perfect. Her Instagram feed was already flooded with the images of her trip so far and had received far more double taps than any of her other altogether mundane photos.

She dived straight in for another refreshing swim, gliding through the crystal waters with ease and attracting covetous looks from the Italian tourists that seemed to have taken over the sunbeds there. When she emerged from the sea, shaking the water from her body like a dog, she lay out and basked on one of the large flat rocks that framed the bay. She dozed whilst the sun worked its magic, drying and tanning her petit swimmer's body at the same time. A short while later, she became aware of the thrum of an engine drawing close, but she chose to ignore it as she was in such a blissful state she didn't want to move.

'Are you coming on an adventure or lying all day on a rock like a savra!' a voice shouted out gleefully. Lifting herself up on her elbows she saw, just a little way out, an enormous Rib, its large double engines purring, holding steady, and Manolis at the wheel grinning like the proverbial Cheshire cat.

'I have no idea what a savra is' she flung back at him, 'but I am for sure having a go in that thing'

She threw her bag to him and then jumped gracefully into the water and swam over to the boat, where he leaned over, offering a strong arm to hoist her in. As he pulled her out of the water and over the side, she impulsively grabbed him and kissed him. He staggered back as she released him, looking dazed and confused, but happy.

'What was that for?' he said, looking at her in amazement and smiling as if he'd won the lotto.

'Just because,' she said flirtily. 'Now, are you going to drive this beast or am I?'

They sped down the coast at high speeds, causing angry tourists to shout and shake fists at them as the wake from the powerful boat caused their smaller 30hp rentals to sway angrily in the aftermath.

Charlotte was in her element, loving the speed, wind whipping her hair wildly and probably making her look like Medusa, but she didn't care. As the sun was setting, Manolis pulled them up to a jetty with practised ease at a beach called Barbati, a long stretch of pebble beach, layered with sunbeds and still busy with prostrate bodies despite the dispersing sun.

'Come,' he said, leaping onto the wooden pier and holding out his hand. 'That place over there, Piedra Del Mare, has the best cocktails on the island, and my cousin Petros works there.'

She ignored his hand and jumped lithely onto the jetty. 'Well, I hope he knows how to make a Paloma' she said, taking his arm as they started to walk towards the beach bar. 'If he doesn't, I'm sure gonna teach him.'

'So what was it you felt the need to go and check earlier, leaving me to be leered at by all those Italians?' she asked as they entered the bar.

'Ah, that wasn't a what, it was a her, and it was my mother I wanted to check on.'

'That's very sweet of you' she smiled at him.

'I don't know if it's sweet, but she needs my support. She suffered from a stroke and struggles to leave the house these days, so I try to pop home whenever I can, although she doesn't enjoy me checking on her. It can be tough for her with the long days I work.'

'God, that's tough for both of you. Do you have other family to help?'

'Yes, we do. My uncle and cousins are all nearby; we're a very close-knit family so they all chip in. She's never left alone for too long'

'That's amazing. I couldn't imagine my family behaving that way. They would rather pay someone to look after anyone who was sick rather than get their hands dirty.'

'Here in Greece we look after our own' said Manolis. 'Family is everything.'

Sitting on the tall bar stools Manolis introduced her to his cousin, a good-looking young man who obviously knew his way around a cocktail shaker, and a short time later he deposited two tall glasses in front of them, rims frosted with salt and slices of grapefruit bobbing in the fizzy orange liquid. Taking a sip, she sighed contentedly. 'That's just perfect, honey,' she said to Petros. 'Come on, Manoli', she added, slipping off her stool. 'Let's go drink these on the beach.'

They sat on a large piece of driftwood by the shore edge and sipped their drinks, watching the red moon rising in awe. 'So how come a little 'ol windsurf instructor like you has got such a kick-ass boat?' she asked unashamedly.

'Ha, I wish,' he replied. 'It belongs to my Uncle Pericles, along with half the island.'

'Pericles, Pericles?' she spluttered, spitting out a mouthful of her drink. 'As in father of Thomas, our pool boy, as in the man that Ms D is currently on a date with?'

'The very same' said Manolis. 'Pericles Salvanos is an extremely rich man, even though he doesn't care to flash it around as some would.'

'Dang, that'll keep her in handbags,' Charlotte snorted, wiping the sticky residue of the cocktail off her tanned legs. Seeing his confused face, she laughed and said, 'don't you worry about it, Manoli' as she had learned to call him. 'Do you fancy a spot of skinny dipping?'

Manolis had no idea what skinny dipping was, but as he followed her along the beach and watched her start to shed her clothes, revealing her perfect body bit by bit, he had a feeling he was going to like it.

SATURDAY

Saturday dawned bright and clear, the seemingly endless blue skies providing the perfect backdrop to the lush, green island. Scott and Linda returned to the villa in time for breakfast, looking sleepy and a little sheepish, the excuse of a broken-down car at the ready, but they needn't have worried.

Everyone seemed to be in a world of their own that morning, barely glancing up as they came through the door holding hands. Charlotte was gazing into space with a small, secret smile on her unmade face whilst Marc seemed intent on his phone, absorbed in messaging with someone.

'How is Tallulah?' Linda enquired after his favourite cat patient, assuming that was what he was checking on.

'What? Um, oh yes, she seems to have pulled through for now,' he said, looking strangely guilty and putting his phone in his pocket. 'How was your evening?' he asked, smiling at the obvious glow his friends had which revealed exactly how their evening had gone.

Just then, Kate came out of her bedroom, dressed and ready to go out and looking particularly glamorous.

'Good morning, Ma. You're a bit eager; the minibus won't be here until 10' Scott said, kissing her on the cheek before sitting next to Linda at the breakfast table.

Smiling at them all, Kate gave a nervous chuckle. 'Actually, I am not coming to the vineyard with ya'll today; I am sure it's going to be wonderful, but I have decided to take up Pericles' offer of a day out on his boat.'

Charlotte choked on her toast; visions of last night's adventures coursing across her mind. The boat had been the scene of a particularly energetic bout of lovemaking. Taking a swig of the freshly squeezed orange juice that Maria had prepared for them she said 'go for it Ms D, you're gonna love the boat, it's the same colour as your tote.' she nodded at the bright red bag slung across the older woman's shoulder.

Kate could feel herself flushing a similar colour to her bag and was relieved to hear the welcome rumble of the motorbike coming down the drive. Who would have believed it possible? A few days ago she would have winced at the roaring, rumbling sound and complained about noise pollution, but now it caused her heart palpitations of the good kind and made her smile until her cheeks hurt.

'You lot behave and make sure you take good care of our guests. The lovely Peter has agreed to go along with y'all to make sure everything runs smoothly.' And with that, she flicked her scarf over her shoulder and walked with as much dignity as she could muster, out of the door and into the waiting arms of Pericles.

Scott's face was a picture. 'Do you think I should be worried?' he asked Linda.

She smiled warmly at him, placing her hand on his thigh causing it to tingle and said, 'I think you should leave her be. I have never seen her look so carefree and happy. Why on earth would you want to interfere with that?'

Marc, who had leapt up like a scalded cat at the mention of Peter's name and was heading down the stairs to get ready, poked his head back up and said 'listen to the girl, Scotty, she's talkin' a whole lot of sense' before continuing down to his room. He felt flustered as never before. He didn't know how he was going to handle today. Yesterday had been so wonderful, probably one of the best days of his life, but he knew it couldn't go on. There was nothing to be gained by pursuing what would only end in tears in a few days when he stepped on the plane to return to his straight-laced life. As he looked at himself in the bathroom mirror, he straightened his back and bolstered his thinking. He knew he would have to pretend as if nothing had happened with Peter; it was the only way he was going to keep his resolve and get through the day.

Charlotte, who had been sat in a daydream, idly twirling her hair, pounced on her phone when it chimed its notification of an incoming message. Avidly reading the text, she lit up like a Christmas tree, squealed excitedly and ran helter-skelter out of the front door, leaving her friends shaking their heads in bemusement.

There in the courtyard, sat astride a large black horse and looking like every fantasy of a cowboy she'd ever had, was Manolis with a cavalier grin on his face. He was holding the reins of a beautiful bay mare that was nibbling at the shrubbery, unconcerned for the sudden appearance of Charlotte who came barrelling out the door and skidding to a halt, grabbing one of the large terracotta urns that framed the entrance for support.

'I thought you might be up for a little more adventure,' he said, grinning wickedly as he swung effortlessly down from his ride.

Charlotte, who'd spent the morning worrying that she had blown the budding relationship by being too forward, her need to feel beautiful and wanted tending to make her jump into the physical side of things a lot quicker than she probably ought, walked slowly towards this man who'd somehow stolen her heart.

'I didn't think I'd see you again,' she murmured into his chest as he enveloped her in his arms, yet again surprised at how open she could be with him. She had never felt comfortable enough in previous relationships to let on how she was really feeling and, as a result, had never become close to her boyfriends, always hiding behind the perfect image that she tried so hard to maintain. He planted a kiss on her head and then held her at arm's length, smiling at her in a way that made her heart sing.

'I have no idea why you would think that. Last night was amazing. You were magical and I don't think it was just because of the four Paloma's you made me drink or the beautiful moon,' he chuckled. 'Besides, I don't think I quite have the knack of skinny dipping yet. You may have to show me again how to do it.'

Filled with a deep joy, she ran back into the villa to get ready. Artlessly tying her hair up and throwing on some clothes without a care, she grabbed her bag, compact left behind without a second thought and bounded back out the door with a speedy 'See y'all later, I'm going out!' before Scott and Linda could react.

Peter, who was edging his car over the lip of the drive to avoid the usual bump to the undercarriage, was startled by the sight of two horses bearing down on him, and it was only as they trotted past that he registered the smiling faces of Charlotte and... Surely that was Manolis from the boat?

He was thankful for the distraction, as he, too, had spent a nervous morning worrying about what would happen next with Marc. Despite the wonderful night they had had which had ended with an incredible, lingering kiss at the door to the villa causing Marc to moan 'Oh God, Petey' when he'd dropped him off, nothing had been said about the future and he was unsure where they now stood. He knew from the conversation they had had that

Marc was terrified of coming out and didn't feel it was possible for him, so where did that leave them?

When Kate had called this morning to ask him to chaperone the group on today's tour, he'd leapt on the chance to spend more time with Marc, but on the drive up the coast, he'd become more and more apprehensive.

He'd called Emma 'Shit, what am I going to do?' he said into his earpiece as he manoeuvred around a hairpin bend.

He knew Marc would behave differently in front of his friends but was hoping for some indication, some sign from the man, that what they had shared last night was something that would be pursued.

'Well, wait and see how he is. You never know. The 'Petey' magnetism may have pushed him out of his shell!' she laughed. 'Failing that, you can message back poor gorgeous George who probably thinks you've forgotten about him by now.'

Not even being able to contemplate spending time with someone else, he dismissed her idea. He knew Emma was just trying to help, let him know there were other fish in the sea, but the only oceans he wanted to gaze into were Marc's incredible blue eyes.

Parking his car at the end of the drive to leave room for the minibus that would be arriving shortly, he grabbed his bag from the footwell and, taking a deep breath, climbed out and strode towards the open door. Finding only Scott and Linda seated on the terrace waiting for him, he exhaled. He hadn't even realised he'd been holding his breath.

'Good morning,' he said as jauntily as possible, pasting a sunny smile on his face. The couple, who'd been deep in conversation and looking very cosy on the rattan sofa, turned around and greeted him.

'Good morning, Peter,' said Scott. 'Are you ready to wrangle this crazy family of mine today? I don't think you know what you've let yourself in for!'

'I'm sure our consummate concierge will handle them as skilfully as he does everything else,' said the dulcet tones of Marc, who'd walked up unnoticed behind them.

Peter whipped around, unsure of what to say or do; he had never been at such a loss in a situation before. Luckily, he was saved from having to respond by the tooting of a horn announcing the arrival of the minibus.

'Ok everyone,' he said, gathering his professional demeanour over him as a shield, 'let's get this show on the road.' And with a fleeting smile at Marc, he marched out the door, leaving the others to follow at their own pace.

Spiros, the driver, greeted them when they boarded the bus. 'Good to see you all again,' he smiled 'I hope you are all enjoying our beautiful island?'

'We certainly are,' said Marc, sitting down near the back. 'Have you always lived here?'

'I spent a short time away when I was a boy' he said, carefully manoeuvring the bus around until he was pointing in the right direction. 'I went to Athens for trials with Olympiacos' he beamed at them. 'You know they are Greece's greatest football team?'

'We don't really watch much soccer,' said Marc, 'but I seem to recall hearing the name. So, what happened, didn't you make the grade?'

'Ha, I most definitely did,' he said, nursing the bus onto the main road. 'They loved me, begged me to play for them, but I couldn't. I couldn't bear to leave Corfu, even with such a reward and prestige as playing for them; it wasn't enough to lure me away!'

Marc and Scott exchanged glances, not entirely convinced by his tale but enjoying his story, anyway.

'Here we are,' announced Spiro as they pulled up outside of the hotel and, opening the door with the push of a button, letting a warm gust of air in with a hiss.

The older members of the group were standing outside of the hotel like a gaggle of cackling geese. Peter was happy to see they were all ready and waiting and leapt off the bus to organise them. 'Good morning, everyone' he smiled at them all. 'Are we ready for today's excursion to the vineyard?'

There was a general muttering of approval amongst the group. Then Uncle Joe put his hand up. 'I need a piss,' he said crudely, causing Aunt Eustace to tut loudly and a flurry of other hands to shoot up as a tidal wave of bladders realised they needed emptying before the hour-long journey.

Eventually, they were all ready. Peter got them seated on the bus and gave Spiros the nod to set off, using his role as a tour guide as an excuse to sit at the front, away from Marc, who seemed to be acting like nothing had happened between them. He picked up the microphone there and started describing the scenery as they travelled to the centre of the island and the Ropa Valley where the vineyard was located.

They were met on arrival by the manager of the Theotoki Estate, owned by one of the oldest families on Corfu. The manor house was set in a verdant valley with fields of vines stretching as far as the eye could see. He gathered them all around and explained the long history of the family and their wines before leading them on the tour, which took in the old house with its remarkable library and collection of ancient maps, before heading to the wine cellars. Here he described the process of winemaking and how it had transformed over the years into the modern techniques used there today in such an enthralling way that even Uncle Joe and his cronies seemed captivated.

After this, they were led out to a shaded courtyard where a table had been set with a magnificent meze of locally produced delicacies and bottles of wine that were lined up to be sampled. Peter organised getting everyone seated and, when he had settled them all, he was most alarmed to see that the one seat free was at the end of the table next to Marc. Biting the bullet, he sat down, smiling nervously in Marc's direction and making a show of ensuring everyone had a glass of wine to taste. He handed out the glasses and told everyone to help themselves and try the different wines.

As the buzz of conversation grew around them, exclamations of enjoyment and opinions of the wines abounding, Peter turned to Marc.

'So, how are you this morning?' he asked cautiously and as casually as he could manage, whilst forking up some Noumboulo, his favourite speciality Corfiot cold cut.

Marc, acting equally nonchalantly, speared a hunk of vine fresh tomato onto his plate and was pointedly not looking at him.

'I'm very good, thank you, Peter,' he said in between mouthfuls of food. 'This place is amazing. Yet again, I'm blown away by the history of Corfu. We sure don't have anything this old at home.'

And with that he turned and started chatting to his neighbour, leaving Peter feeling wretched and with no other choice than to turn his attention to Scott and Linda, whose close headed conversation seemed to have erupted into some kind of heated debate.

'I'm sorry, Scotty, but this is important to me. It's something that I have to do,' she was saying seriously.

'I can't believe after everything you would, without warning, announce that you're going to head off and travel the world for a year as if last night didn't mean anything, as if I don't mean anything!' Scott responded, his voice rising in anger, looking at her like she was completely irrational.

Peter pushed his chair back quickly and stood up.'I'm just going to take another look at the wine cellars,' he announced to an oblivious audience and made a quick exit from the untenable situation developing around him at the table.

Linda took Scott's hand and looked earnestly at him, trying to find the words to explain what was in her heart.

'This trip has been wonderful and has made me realise something, Scott. You should follow your dreams, your heart. And my dream is to travel, to see as much as possible before I settle down, and I know if I don't do it now I never will.'

'That may be your dream, but what about your heart? I thought you loved me?' He said, pulling his hand away, his face contorted with shock and pain.

'I do love you, Scott; I can't imagine my life without you. But when we get back to the villa, I am booking a different flight from Athens. I'm going to start a journey I have been planning for years. Why don't you come with me?' She asked, leaning forward, eyes wide, fuelled by the sudden sense of freedom her decisions had given her.

Scott looked into the beautiful face of the woman he adored, torn. He would love nothing more than to head off with her into the sunset to who knows where. He didn't care as long as they were together, but he had commitments. He could well imagine his father's reaction if he announced he was throwing in the towel at the firm for a nomad lifestyle with this woman he knew his Pa didn't, in reality, approve of. And then there was his mother, who relied so heavily on him for support. She would never be able to cope left by herself. It wasn't feasible. As much as the idea of escaping it all appealed to him, he couldn't imagine ever being able to break loose from the various holds on him. He shook his head sadly, gazing down at the table, not focusing on anything but the ball of pain welling up inside him, unable to imagine a life without Linda.

Peter, who was leaning on the cool walls of the wine cellar, felt a bit stupid. Stupid for hiding in here, stupid for thinking a gorgeous man like Marc would fall in love with him and he would find his prince charming, and stupid for agreeing to come on today's excursion. He banged his head against the wall. 'Stupid, stupid, stupid,' he muttered, punctuating each word with a connection with the ancient stones, not caring if he left a bruise on his forehead.

'Am I interrupting something?' said Marc from the arched doorway. He had realised that he was behaving like a complete bastard to Peter, basically treating him the same as all the girls he had pretended to go out with before, and he wasn't keen on the feeling it left him with. He decided to risk tracking Peter down. He needed to see him, to explain how he was feeling; but he had to make sure nobody overheard them.

'I was just berating myself for thinking you would actually find me attractive,' said Peter honestly, despite being so embarrassed at having been caught acting like some kind of lunatic.

'I think you know after last night that I do find you attractive,' Marc responded, causing both of them to have flashbacks to the final, lingering kiss goodnight.

'The thing is, Peter, I can't come out. There's no way my family is going to accept that I am gay. My father would disown me and my brothers would probably beat the crap out of me and dump me in Buffalo Bayou.'

'This is no way to live your life' said Peter seriously, walking over to Marc and putting his hand on his shoulder, trying to ignore the frisson of excitement even that small point of contact sparked. Putting his feelings aside, he felt he had to help Marc come to terms with his situation.

'Are you going to spend your whole life pretending to be something you're not, hiding who you are and who you love?'

'I have managed pretty well so far,' he said ruefully. 'Yesterday was a bit of holiday madness. Corfu seems to have affected us all in some way. I will always treasure the time we had together, but the truth is that in 48 hours I will be on a plane and heading back to reality, so I need to prepare myself for that.'

At that moment, the manager walked in. He'd come to collect some more wine as the table was running dry already. 'Everything alright gentlemen?' he asked as the two men jumped apart guiltily.

'Yes, yes,' Peter said hurriedly. 'Can I help you with those?' he added as the manager started to pick up a selection of bottles and rushed over to take a few from his overburdened hands. Marc stood by dejectedly, watching them as they walked back out to the courtyard, carefully carrying the precious cargo. He waited in the cool of the cellar, listening to the sounds of festivities from outside echoing around the solid brick walls and reverberating for a while, before collecting himself together and walking back out into the brilliant sunshine which acutely emphasized the darkness he felt inside.

The drive back to the villa in the minibus was torture for the two younger couples seated near the front of the minibus, gazing out of the windows from their individual seats in an attempt to alleviate the agony of the nightmare ride.

The older members of the party, after practically buying up the whole shop at the vineyard, had loaded the bus with cases of wine along with various local products. The air was redolent with stale alcohol, spicy salamis and pungent cheeses, all being circulated by the air conditioning unit that was working overtime in the extreme heat, spewing a trail of water out on the road behind it as it climbed back over the mountains.

The not so venerable ones were obviously feeling a little homesick now in their inebriated states. Singing wildly, out of tune and tempo, they had murdered The Yellow Rose of Texas and Amarillo by Morning, and now they were tearfully warbling their way through Texas, Our Texas. Even Great Aunt Eustace had joined in with that one, despite feeling travel sick and spending most of the journey with her face in a paper bag and adding to the pungency of the bus.

The hour-long trip back to the hotel seemed to last forever, a Groundhog Day of repetitive bends and warbling, but the silence that descended after the old folk got off made the further few minutes to the villa interminable.

Kate, however, was having an entirely different experience on this penultimate day of the holiday. Pericles had whisked her off on another thrilling bike ride up the coast to a small harbour on the other side of Kassiopi called Imerolia.

'Guess which boat is mine?' he asked, similar to a child looking for praise for doing something clever, as they walked over to the quayside. Kate had to laugh. Even if Charlotte hadn't already given the game away by telling her the colour of the boat, she would have guessed straight away. There, sitting sleekly, nestled between all the small, well used looking fishermen's crafts, was a beast of a boat which, even to her untrained eyes, spoke of power and speed and, above all, money.

After settling her in and making sure she was comfortable, Pericles started the powerful engines, and they made their way surprisingly sedately out of the harbour. Once they had reached a point he clearly felt was appropriate, he opened up the throttle, and they sped north. The force of the propulsion pushed her back into the leather seat and it felt as if they were gliding across the sea, almost flying above the waves. The speed and the noise made it impossible to talk but, as they came around the top of Corfu and started to approach another, smaller island where there was more traffic, he slowed down to make way for the various vessels and they could talk.

'This is Ericoussa,' he told her. 'The first of the three Diapontia Islands, which is the most Western point of Greece.'

'You're not going to tell me you own these too, are you? Who are you, Aristotle Onassis?'

He laughed at her sassiness, a constant source of amusement to him along with her primness, and said 'no I don't own any islands, but my uncle does have a taverna on that little island over there, Mathraki. That's where we are aiming for.'

With that he revved up the engines again and, a short while later, they were motoring, gently now, into a tiny harbour where a wiry, sun-weathered old man was waiting to field the ropes thrown to him, surrounded by cats that seemed to think they would be bringing in fish.

'Ignore these greedy bastards' he shouted in greeting, his face creased up in a smile. 'They have eaten enough to sink Mobey Dick this morning, but still they ask for more!'

They spent a pleasant hour drinking espresso on the terrace of the waterside taverna with Uncle Thanasis. Despite living hermit-like on this tiny island with barely 300 residents, he seemed to be up to date on all the local gossip over on Corfu, which was as far as his world seemed to stretch. Kate couldn't imagine living here; it was so completely distant from her life back in Houston.

'So how is life going with the new lady mayor?' he asked Pericles with a slight smirk on his face 'I hear she has been cleaning up in true female fashion!'

'You may laugh,' said Pericles quite seriously, 'but so far, she's doing a hell of a job. She's got the rubbish moving, streets and squares are being cleaned and she's even had markings painted on all the roads where there are schools.'

Kate listened with interest. She'd heard that there had been a problem with the removal of refuse off the island and had been pleasantly surprised when she arrived to see very little evidence of this. In fact, she had noticed many recycling centres as they had driven around, which she had found impressive on such a small island.

'It sounds to me like she's doing a great job,' she said. 'Was it her that organised the recycling centres I've seen?

Pericles smiled at her.'no, they are run by volunteers. The one good thing to come out of the rubbish crisis, it became a catalyst and made people living here realise they had to be responsible for their island. Greeks and foreigners alike work side by side every week to help transform this place.'

'Well, from what you say, she's off to a good start *despite* being a woman,' she said pointedly, looking at the old man, who laughed.

'As the great man said, "Quality is not an act, it is a habit". Let's see how she does after this honeymoon period. If she's still scrubbing the streets in a year's time rather than sleeping on the stacks of money stolen from the masses like all the other bastards in office, then I shall applaud her. Hell, I'll bow down and kiss her feet!'

'That I'd pay to see,' said Pericles, slapping his uncle affectionately on the back.

'Right, we should be off,' he said as he stood up.

'What's your rush?' smirked Thanasis. 'Wait a moment, I'll get your hamper but you must have some Tsipouro before you go,' and he hobbled back into the taverna with surprising speed.

Kate looked inquiringly at Pericles, 'do I want to drink this Tsipouro?'

'If you haven't tried it yet, you should. It's fine, it's made from grapes, so it's good for you,' he said, and laughed at her expression of doubt.

Thanasis came bounding back out. He was remarkably spritely for an old man, carrying a basket in one hand and balancing a tray containing three small glasses filled with a clear liquid skilfully on the other. Setting the basket on the floor, he put the tray on the table and placed the glasses in front of Kate and Pericles before taking the third one and raising it in a toast. 'To family, love and friendships' he said and knocked back the drink in one go.

'Here, here,' said Kate, following suit, the fiery liquid burning the back of her throat as it went down and leaving an afterglow in her stomach. Eyes watering, she watched as Pericles did the same and banged his glass down on the table with a resounding thud.

'Come on Miss Kate, we have other things to do today apart from keeping this old man company.' And, hugging his uncle, he picked up the wicker hamper and held his hand out to Kate. He led her away from the taverna along a rough, narrow track that ran along the shoreline until they reached a small, unspoiled beach, where he placed the basket down and began to set everything up.

He had thought of everything for their day, from a rug to lie on, towels to dry themselves, an umbrella to shade them to the basket, which was filled with food and drinks for them to enjoy. Nothing had been left to chance and Kate was beginning to realise exactly how special this man was.

She had always been the one who organised things; thought of everyone else's needs and looked after them, so now to have someone who thought about her first was a complete epiphany. She was surprised to find herself enjoying this reversal of roles and being on the receiving end of special treatment for a change.

They made leisurely forays into the sea, swimming through the brilliantly clear waters that sparkled with the reflection of the sun overhead. He amused her with his antics, showing off and jumping off the nearby rocks to impress her, splashing her at every available opportunity. Again, she was struck by the childlike nature of Pericles. His pure enjoyment in the here and now was wondrous to her. He didn't appear to have a care in the world.

When they tired of swimming, they collapsed on the blanket laid out under the umbrella and dove into the feast provided by Thanasis. Stuffed vine leaves, tiny meatballs tasting of fresh herbs and slices of a hard, salty cheese called Graviera all were washed down with a delicious white wine. It was all wonderful, the food, the company and the ambience, and she was amazed yet again at how comfortable she felt in these new surroundings and situations. She couldn't remember the last time she's spent time alone with a man, probably before Scott was born if she thought about it, and that was an awfully long time to be without this intimate companionship.

She lay back after their feast whilst he put away the remains of their meal, more content than she could ever recall feeling, and she dozed off for a while. She eventually became aware of a shadow over her and opened her eyes to see the smiling face of Pericles inches away from her; she could smell the garlic from the meatballs on his breath and see the crystals of salt from sea on his forehead where the sun had dried his skin.

'Do you need anything else?' he asked, his sultry voice and the proximity of his body firing her libido instantly, an astounding awakening of senses, more dizzying after years of enforced dormancy, and a tidal wave of lust ran through her body.

'Well, there is one thing I need' she replied and, with that, pulled him towards her until their lips met and they kissed, hesitantly at first, gradually becoming more ferocious until they devoured each other, both of them relishing in the touch and intimacy that had been missing from their lives for so long.

Charlotte, despite her saddle sore behind, was enjoying herself thoroughly. Manolis had taken them on a path that ran around the headland between Avlaki and San Stefanos. Erimitis was a nature reserve and, as they pushed through the overgrown paths, they were delighted by butterflies and metal coloured dragonflies, sunlight glinting off their wings, visiting the wildflowers which grew so abundantly there.

He showed her around the lake and then led them down to a small cove, a tiny patch of sand that seemed to be untouched by humans. Here they tethered the horses and she once again demonstrated the art of skinny dipping. They frolicked happily in the sea before falling on the sun-warmed sand together, totally lost in each other's bodies.

That is, until they were interrupted by a group of startled German tourists who were obviously on a serious hike, judging by the amount of equipment they had with them. Laughing so hard that her shoulders were shaking into the towel hastily placed to cover their dignity, she watched the tutting hikers move on down the beach, casting disapproving glances back at them. Charlotte, as the giggles subsided, looked at Manolis, who was still wiping tears from his eyes.

'I don't know whether it's you or the magic of Corfu but I have never felt so utterly...' she paused, her face screwed up as she searched for the word 'Me.' she finally came up with 'do you understand what I mean?'

'I think I do,' he replied, having learnt a little of her family and the way they had always pushed her. 'Corfu is a place where people find themselves, and I think you have for the first time let your true inner nature out to play.' He added before being drawn back in by the seductive nipple that had been playfully peeking out at him from the side of the towel.

Back at the villa, they had all dispersed to the solitude of their rooms. As he stood under the shower, Marc cursed himself and his life, the powerful jets unable to wipe the image of Peter's hurt face as he said goodbye to them. He had longed to throw his arms around the man and comfort him, but had restrained himself, nodding a curt goodbye before going into the villa. He had to be strong, just one more day to go and he could get back to his life, his carefully ordered life where lovely blonde concierges didn't exist and everybody thought he was a playboy. He leaned his head against the tiled wall, letting the water beat down on him in an attempt to wash away his sorrow.

In the adjacent room, in an almost mirror image of his friend, Scott stood under his shower, hoping for a similar effect, but it seemed that the magic of Corfu didn't extend to its waters have the cleansing abilities of Lourdes and, as he towelled himself dry, he was still anguished. How could Linda do this to him? The night they had spent at the apartment in the village had been so wonderful. They had had the most intense sex he had ever experienced and he thought that they had connected on a new, profound level.

To now discover she'd had a yen to travel the world harboured away inside her since she was a child and he had had no idea, was making him think that maybe he didn't know this girl at all. Maybe it was better that she had said no to him on the jetty and was going to disappear from his life. Who knew what other secrets she had kept from him. Feeling righteously spurned, he felt better equipped to deal with the next few days and the rest of his life. Being angry at her made it a whole lot easier, but why did it seem so empty without her?

Of the three, Linda was in the best frame of mind. Her shower had refreshed her and, as she sat on the terrace outside of her room, sipping her water and excitedly tapping away on her laptop, she felt at peace. Of course, she knew she had hurt Scott, which was the last thing that she had ever wanted to do. But being here had been a catalyst for the plan that had been bubbling away inside her for such a long time.

She had inherited her desire to travel from her mother, who had single-handedly raised her in their tiny apartment in the ironically named Sunnyside area of Houston. In a neighbourhood renowned for its high crime rate and low rent properties, Camila had created a home for them, plastering the walls with posters of foreign countries and cities and telling her daughter stories of other cultures and worlds which seemed enchanting to Linda as a small girl.

Her mother had worked hard at two menial cleaning jobs to provide food for the table, and what she had scrimped and saved went towards Linda's college when she had decided to be a nail technician. When Linda had graduated, her mother had presented her with the St. Christopher necklace she still wore today. It was her most treasured possession. Linda had been determined to take her mother to all the wonderful places they had dreamed of, but her plans had been dashed when her mother died five years ago from a heart attack. That was when she started collecting her tips in her 'possibilities pot', determined then to do the travelling Camila had never managed to do.

When Scott had tried to propose on that fateful jetty, she had felt a switch flick inside her. Kate Delaney's neurotic tendencies aside, she knew there and then she wasn't ready to settle down, that it was now or never before she became tied up in married life, buying a house, maybe having kids and saving for their futures. She had to make a break, despite the deep bond she had with Scott. If he wasn't willing to come with her or wait for her, then it was a chance she had to take. She owed it to Camila and the dreams she had held in check all her life for her daughter's sake, and she owed it to herself to go and explore the wonderful places that had adorned the walls of her childhood home.

Peter had stopped off at a bar called Dirty Nellie's in the resort of Ipsos on his way back home and sat, if not crying into his beer, then certainly depressing it with his miserable face. He felt completely isolated from the revelry going on around him, as groups of young holidaymakers downed cocktails of lurid colours and inappropriate names. As he sat in the corner watching the happy faces around him, the reflection of the neon bar sign flashing different colours across his shirt, he realised he had to make a decision.

As much as he loved his life here in Corfu, he had been becoming aware that maybe he had outgrown it. Being here in a couple, he had made a good life for himself. He had a great circle of friends and a job he loved. But being here by himself, even with all that going for him, was a lonely existence and something had to give.

He had tentatively been looking at jobs back in England in the months leading up to the Delany party's arrival, and he knew without a doubt that some of the emails he had received in response to his applications would lead to a job. But none of these had felt quite right. The thought of returning to the 9-5 existence filled him with dread, and he realised he needed to look further afield to find something that he would enjoy somewhere where he could be himself. So far the right situation hadn't presented itself.

The glimpse of love he had seen with Marc was now galvanising his resolve to move on. He knew now that he couldn't continue the way things were and, in order to make changes in his life, he had to change himself and his mind-set. It seemed he had become stuck in yet another rut, and it was time to force his way out. Downing the last of his beer and leaving some coins on the table, he went back to his car, his mind racing with possibilities as he drove home to feed his cats.

Manolis had taken Charlotte home to meet his mother, another instinctive reaction to this rollercoaster few days with her. He hadn't called ahead to warn her and when they walked in to find her still sitting on her balcony, still in her nightgown, cloaked in the darkness, she was none too pleased with him.

'Why are you bringing guests to our home without telling me?' Alexandra muttered to him in Greek.

'Forgive me, mama, I thought you would enjoy some company,' he replied honestly as he helped her stand up to meet Charlotte.

Alexandra pulled herself up and put out her left hand to the girl. Charlotte, who knew that the woman had very little strength in her right side now, didn't bat an eyelid and took her hand in hers.

'I am very pleased to meet you, Mrs Mavromatis,' she said, smiling at her.

'And I you, but I am not so pleased to be sitting here in my night things, with nothing to offer you! My son should be more thoughtful towards his mother and his guest.'

'Don't you worry about that' Charlotte replied, understanding completely how the woman must feel caught unawares, not ready to be seen. 'If you would feel better, why don't you go and get yourself dressed, but please don't feel you had to on my account. Look at me, I look like nine miles of bad road!'

Alexandra nodded, gave a brief smile and made her way slowly towards her bedroom; she stopped, looking over her shoulder with a whisper of a grin.

'You must look like pretty much every road in Corfu then!' she said playfully and, laughing at her own joke, continued into her room.

'Right, Manoli, let's organise some food out here. Your poor mother obviously feels dreadful not being able to offer us anything,' she scolded him. Laughing at her mock telling off, he walked over to the kitchen area and pulled out various containers from the fridge.

'We always have food. Uncle Pericles makes sure we have something every day from the taverna, and to be honest, my mum doesn't eat very much. All her appetites seem to have disappeared in these last years,' he added, looking more sombre.

She went over and hugged him before helping him set out what they needed for the table on the balcony, then starting to reheat the delicious-looking food, finding her way around the small kitchen easily.

When Alexandra came back out, it was to a scene glowing with cosiness and filled with laughter and delicious smells. Charlotte stood by the stove stirring several pots and Manolis was lighting citronella candles on the balcony to ward off the mosquitoes and they were giggling over some comment or other.

Her house suddenly seemed like a home, which it hadn't done for years, and made her smile. Charlotte, seeing Alexandra appear, naturally went over and took the woman's arm and walked with her to the table where Manolis pulled out a chair for her, chattering all the way.

'Mrs Mavromatis, you have such a lovely home,' she was saying. 'I absolutely love the view from your balcony; you can watch the whole village from here and see the sea right there.'

'It is a wonderful house my Pericles has created for me' she smiled at the girl. 'And please, call me Alexandra.'

Manolis was beaming with happiness. His mother was looking more animated than he'd seen her in such a long time; it had been so hard to watch her gradually fading away. The vibrant, always laughing woman that he'd known as a boy had ebbed away leaving a fragile shell, and it pained him to see her day after day, staring out to sea unsmiling for hours on end despite his best efforts to draw her out.

'I hope you are hungry, mama,' he said, indicating the feast spread out before her, moving some dishes aside as Charlotte brought a plate of toasted pitta bread to add to the already overburdened table.

'I think I can manage a little,' she said, surprised to find herself feeling a little hungry. 'Manoli, mou, why don't you bring some of our wine? If we are doing this, we should do it properly!'

Grinning even wider, he jumped up to respond to her request, feeling like the luckiest man in the world. He couldn't believe a girl like Charlotte would ever look at a boy like him, but here she was, in his home, chatting away with his mother, whose eyes were sparkling in the candlelight. As he took a bottle of their last year's wine from the top cupboard in the kitchen, he offered up a silent prayer of thanks to whichever gods might be listening.

When Pericles arrived home late that night, he was very surprised to see the lights still on in his sister's house and the sound of laughter and music coming from the balcony. As intrigued as he was, the sight of Thomas's Vespa reminded him that he had more pressing things to talk of with his son. When he walked in, he found Thomas lounged on the sofa, feet up on the coffee table, watching his favourite series on Netflix.

'Turn that off son, I need to talk to you.' he said as he hung his coat up behind the front door. Turning around to see that the boy hadn't shifted, he strode over and snatched the remote out of his hand and hit the off button. 'I said I need to talk to you, I'm serious.'

'What now, dad. I said thank you for going to the villa for me. What more do you want?' he said, standing and walking to the fridge and taking out two bottles of beer. As he placed them on the counter and pulled open the drawer to find the opener, Pericles watched him, unsure where to start and even less sure where to finish.

'I want to talk to you about women,' he finally came up with. Thomas flushed, pushing his fringe out of his eyes and taking a long pull from the now open bottle. 'It's a bit late to tell me about the birds and the bees,' he grinned, passing his father his beer. Taking it gratefully, Pericles chuckled. 'That is definitely not what I meant,' he laughed. 'I guess I just wanted to let you know that I was wrong. I have been wrong for many years, bad-mouthing every woman on the planet to you because of how your mother behaved.' Thomas looked at him while continuing to drink.

'Go on,' he said simply.

Pericles was unsure what else to add. How could you undo years of negativity in one small sentence? 'I am trying to let you know that not all women are bad, in the same way not all men are bad, or all dogs for that matter.' Warming to his subject, he went, 'just because you get bitten once doesn't mean you'll never have another dog, right?' he looked hopefully at the boy, looking for signs that his message was getting through.

A smile split his son's face 'I'm glad to hear you say these things' he said sheepishly. 'You see, I have been talking to someone, a girl. You know Eleni from the car hire shop?'

'Of course I know her, Stamatis' daughter, great girl,' said Pericles, smiling. 'So have you taken her out?'

'God no, I have only recently managed to say Kalimera to her, dad, it has taken weeks to get that far!'

Pericles shook his head, laughing. 'Oh my poor boy, what have I done to you? I tell you what, tomorrow when you see her, ask her out. You can bring her to the restaurant.'

'No offence, dad but if I take her out, I am not taking her somewhere you and the rest of the family can stand gawping at us all night. But you're right, I should ask her. No time like the present, huh?'

'Exactly! As a friend of mine would say, "grab the bull by the horns", get yourself over there tomorrow.' He raised his bottle. 'Here's to seizing the day,' he said, and Thomas joined the toast, happy to see his father so relaxed after telling him about Eleni. He'd been dreading bringing up the subject and was glad it was out in the open.

'Now, let's go next door and see what my sister is up to. It's not usual for her to be up at this time,' said Pericles, finishing his beer and placing the bottle on the draining board.

He was surprised to find his sister and nephew sitting around the table on the balcony with a beautiful young girl who was animatedly chatting with Alexandra, their faces glowing in the candlelight. Thomas registered who it was and stopped in his tracks, afraid to confront the vivacious young woman who had messaged him two nights before. Looking up from the conversation, Manolis jumped up.

'Uncle Pericles,' he said, walking over to hug him. 'I'd like to introduce you to Charlotte.' She stood up to join them. 'Pleased to meet you,' she said formally but found herself unexpectedly embraced in a bear hug.

'It's a pleasure to meet anyone who can put a smile on my sister's face,' he said, releasing her and beaming at Alexandra. He turned and saw his son hovering in the doorway, the consternation was written all over him and the penny dropped. He laughed. 'come on in son, she won't bite you.'

Thomas edged his way in nervously and Charlotte walked over and stood in front of him. Embarrassed as she had been over messaging him, she now didn't give a hoot.

'Honey, I have to apologise for the other night. I wasn't in my right mind. I hope we can laugh it off.'

Thomas was flooded with relief. As gorgeous as the girl was, she was too much for him. He was more attracted to someone, a little more traditional. He didn't have the experience of dealing with someone so upfront. Still feeling uncomfortable, he nodded and forced himself to smile at her to show no hard feelings and went over to kiss his aunt.

'Come, sit and join us,' said Alexandra enthusiastically. 'We have some food left and of course plenty of wine.' So they all sat down, squeezing around the small table, laughing and talking into the small hours.

SUNDAY

On the last morning of their holiday, it was five very different people who met at the breakfast table. They had all started out with their individual ideas of how the week would be and their expectations of it, and they had all been resoundingly knocked for six by the events that had taken place. It had been nothing like they thought it would be, yet everything that they had needed. The island was blessed with a magical air that brought a new perspective to every day and an underlying sense of freedom that had catapulted them all in new directions.

Kate had come to Corfu looking for nothing more than validation. Validation in her ability to organise a trip by herself and, of course, the 'perfect' proposal. Instead, she had found love of a kind she hadn't believed possible until a few short days ago. When she thought about Pericles, which she did often, her heart leapt, bursting with love. Then her brain reminded her of the situation and her heart sank again. It was a never-ending rollercoaster for the poor organ; how it was still calmly beating she didn't know, but it was ready for the next thrilling surge of emotion.

She was sitting, as ever, at the head of the table and, despite her inner turmoil, was aware of the subdued demeanour of the younger generation sitting around her. Charlotte was off in a world of her own, smiling to herself and humming a tune Kate annoyingly couldn't quite recognise. She was looking particularly pretty this morning, Kate thought as she watched the girl sipping her coffee.

She looked different somehow; maybe it was the suntan. Whatever it was, she noticed the girl seemed extremely happy and Kate was thrilled to see her looking this way.

Sitting opposite her was Marc, who was looking positively glum; his usually cheerful face was a picture of misery and, for the world, she couldn't imagine what had brought him so low; he had seemed positively glowing the morning before. But now he looked as if he had all the world's problems on his shoulders and was barely responding to any of the conversation going on around him, which was so unlike him. He could usually be relied on to be the life and soul of any gathering, but now he sat mutely, pushing his untouched food around the plate.

As for her Scotty, his frowning face and stilted requests to pass the toast reminded her of when he was a child, sulking because he didn't get his way. Judging by the steely looks he was giving Linda, she was surely the root of this tantrum, even though the girl seemed positively perky and had a determined set to her jaw that Kate hadn't noticed before. She had hoped their trips together over the last couple of days would have sealed the rift between them, but it would seem not. She sighed. She knew there was nothing she could or should do, other than let them sort it out by themselves.

'So, how was the vineyard yesterday?' she asked. Having got in after midnight, she hadn't had the chance to speak to any of them and was hoping to break the silence that had fallen on the table.

'It was great, Ma, if you don't mind being jilted and then serenaded by a bus full of ol' fools who should know better at their age!' Scott snapped, pushing back his chair and storming down to his room, his resolve to be cool, calm and collected failing at the first hurdle.

They all looked at Linda in surprise; none of them had taken in the events of yesterday, being too wrapped up in their own personal sagas to notice the rift between the couple. Linda looked back at them, various emotions playing across her face before settling back into the determined set of moments before. She looked around the table before starting to speak.

'Kate, I appreciate everything you've done for me, particularly this holiday. It has meant the world to me. But I won't be travelling back with you tomorrow. In fact, when Peter arrives, I am going to be asking him to book me a taxi for this evening. You see, I've decided to go travelling.'

Linda gulped at this point; aware of her feelings overloading as she at long last admitted her plans out loud, her precious necklace in danger of being yanked off, she was twisting it so hard.

'It's always been my dream to travel, you see,' she went on to explain hesitatingly to the stunned faces around her, 'and now I feel is the time to do it. I know Scotty is all shaken up over it but I'm hoping he'll get over it, and just maybe when I get back he will have forgiven me enough to try again, but I have to go.' And, emotions inexorably reaching their peak, she burst into tears which were as much joy for the adventure ahead as sadness for what she was leaving behind.

Charlotte instantly leapt up and went to her friend, holding her close and allowing the tears to soak into her t-shirt.

'Good for you!' exclaimed Kate, to everyone's amazement. 'I wish I'd had the guts to do something like that before I settled down. Scotty will get over it and, if he's got any sense, he'll love you even more for it,' she stated. 'You have to follow your heart.'

Linda was blown away by the woman's response. She had expected fireworks and accusations and her fierce defence of Scott's wellbeing, as always, not this positive affirmation of her plans. It made her feel stronger in her decision. Seeing Scott's face as he stormed off had momentarily cast doubts in her mind, but she knew now it was more because she didn't want to hurt him, not because she didn't believe she should go.

'Thank you, Kate, it means the world to me that you of all people understand why I am doing this.' she smiled at the older woman. 'It hasn't been an easy decision, what with everything that has happened this week, and I certainly don't take the decision lightly. But I do know it's the right one for me.'

Charlotte gave her another tight squeeze. It made perfect sense to her that her friend would want to throw off her shackles after everything she had been feeling recently. As much as she'd thought of them as the golden couple, she had come to see that they wanted different things in life, for now anyway, and she was pleased that Linda was doing something about it rather than settling. It made her own decision seem less impulsive.

'Well, as it's revelation time,' said Charlotte over the top of Linda's head, 'I won't be travelling with you tomorrow either, Kate. I'm going to spend the rest of the summer here with Manolis and see where things lead,' she announced with glee, looking like the cat that'd got the cream.

She had talked it through with Manolis and his mother at the end of their evening together and both of them had been delighted, for different reasons. The idea was met with resounding approval from Pericles as well, although Thomas had looked a little shell-shocked. As far as Pericles was concerned, anyone who made his sister light up and do more than just stare morosely out to sea was more than welcome, and Charlotte had been made to feel part of the family, something she had never felt in her own household.

The swim school didn't start up again for a couple of months, so she figured she had nothing to lose. She usually filled the summer months working at a café, but the idea of spending it here in the sunshine with that gorgeous man was much more appealing.

Linda, who had just finished drying her tears on her friend's top, smiled up at her. 'I'm so happy for you, Lotte,' she said. 'It's more than time that you had a real love and I have never seen you as happy as this before.'

And they could all see the difference in Charlotte. Gone were the layers of makeup, the carefully chosen outfits and shoes to be replaced by a relaxed, carefree girl who looked even more beautiful in her natural state than she ever had gussied up to the nines. She looked positively luminous.

'Good for you' said Kate yet again. 'It seems like Corfu has had a striking effect on all of us.' And teasing looked expectantly at Marc. 'Well, young man, have you got anything to add?' she asked smilingly. Marc hesitated a beat, looking as if he was going to add something before saying 'no ma'am, situation normal here, I will be coming home as expected.'

To which they all laughed and started to clear away the breakfast things, talking animatedly about the girls' new plans as they carried the plates through to the kitchen, where Maria was bustling around cleaning up.

Unnoticed by anyone but Marc, Peter stood in the doorway looking completely lost and forlorn. Their eyes locked together for a long moment, unspoken words flying through the air faster than light, each of them desperate for the other to understand. Marc felt a building up of pressure inside him until irrevocably something snapped; he stood up abruptly and blurted out 'I'm gay!'

The girls, who were all standing by the sink with Maria helping to load up the dishwasher, turned around slowly with various looks on their faces, each of them taking in what he'd said in their own way. Kate and Linda looked amazed, whilst Charlotte had a look of understanding brightening her face.

'I am gay,' he repeated. 'I have always been gay and I always will be and I don't care who knows it,' he added, sounding somewhat hysterical and feeling light-headed. He looked across at Peter, who was still standing in the doorway but now with a huge grin on his face, nodding his approval.

'Well butter my butt and call me a biscuit. Thank fuck for that!' exclaimed Charlotte. 'Sorry Miss D,' she added automatically. 'All these years I thought there was something wrong with me and there was; I'm a girl!' and she fell about laughing uproariously, doubled up in amusement.

Kate and Linda, who were a little less self-centred and realised the implications of what he had told them, gathered around to give him a group hug, reaching around his broad frame and holding him close.

'Well, you sure 'nuff kept that under your hat' said Kate, although things were certainly clicking into place in her head, his seemingly playboy antics now telling an entirely different story.

'Have you told your family?' asked Linda, looking up at him in concern. She knew enough of his background and couldn't imagine this fact being welcome on the homestead.

Visibly paling at the thought, he shook his head vigorously. 'That pleasure awaits me when I get back home,' he said. 'It ain't gonna be pretty but it has to be done' and extracting himself from the ladies he walked over to where Peter was still standing, saying as he went 'as a wise man told me yesterday, I can't spend my whole life pretending to be something I'm not, hiding who I am and who I love' and with that planted a huge kiss on Peter's wonderful smiling face.

Later that day, watching Peter and Marc sitting by the pool dangling their feet in the water and chatting away, leaning into each other, so obviously enrapt, Kate couldn't help but smile. After the initial shock, the news had settled over her quite comfortably. She had always known the boy was a little at odds with his surroundings, and now she understood why. She did feel immense sorrow that it had taken him until now to be comfortable enough to declare himself, but she was happy that he had.

'They're like salt'n'pepper pots' she said over the music that Linda had put on, which she noticed included tracks such as The Passenger and We've Gotta Get Out of This Place. Considering the playlists had been made before they arrived, she wondered if the girl was aware her subconscious had been very much in charge of selecting her songs for the journey.

Linda was shuffling through her boarding passes and stuffing what few clothes she was planning to take with her into a backpack, leaving the rest with Charlotte to mind until she knew when she was going to return, whenever that may be.

She looked up and could see exactly what Kate meant. Physically, they were equally matched; they were both tall with broad shoulders, but Marc's thick, wavy black hair and blue eyes contrasted with Peter's fine blonde locks and warm brown eyes, making them look mismatched yet perfectly matched at the same time.

'It's wonderful to finally see Marc so happy,' Linda said. 'It's hard to imagine spending all those years denying who you are,' she added thoughtfully, looking at the older woman. 'So, what about you, Kate? Your advice to me to follow my heart sounds like something I should say to you.'

Shaking her head sadly, Kate smiled at this young girl who had become so important to her in this last week. 'I have left it too late, Linda. That's why I admire what you are doing so much. We are both walking away from love but it is for very different reasons. Yours is a much braver journey. I am merely going back to what's safe, the familiar.'

'But what about Pericles? Don't you want to see where that might go? I've seen you together. You can't tell me you're not in love, it's written all over your face every time his name gets mentioned. Look, there it goes again!' said Linda laughing and pointing at Kate's face, which had lit up at the sound of his name.

Kate shook her head and waved a hand dismissively, 'I have too much invested in Houston and he has too much invested here, it's not practical for either of us to go globetrotting for love's sake at our time of life' she said, not wanting to point out that Scotty was going to need her now much more than she needed him. It was going to take him some time to recover from this abandonment, however right the girl was heading off into the sunset.

She knew he would need her support to get through these next few months while he came to terms with what she could tell he saw as a betrayal. She only hoped he would heal faster than she did when Danial had left, and not let this colour the rest of his life as she had so stupidly done.

'Make sure you stay in touch,' Kate said, looking at her seriously. 'Wherever you are, please take a couple of minutes to send me an email. I shall be watching your adventures with great interest.'

Linda, feeling on the verge of tears yet again, put her backpack aside and gave Kate a hug. 'Of course I will, you don't get rid of me that easily' she laughed, sniffing and wiping her eyes on a hastily grabbed tissue.

As requested, Peter had booked Linda's taxi for 6 pm, in time for the evening flight to Athens, from where she was jetting off to Sri Lanka, her first port of call on her new journey. Everyone apart from Scott gathered to say goodbye. She had tried to talk to him earlier, but he wasn't having any of it, answering her in short, stilted sentences that led the conversation nowhere, so eventually she gave up.

'Scott, please talk to me,' she'd said from the doorway of his bedroom, not feeling she had the right any more to walk in, uninvited. 'I don't want to leave things like this.'

But he had just looked angrily at her. 'Tough, this is how it is,' he'd snarled, before turning away and refusing to say anything else.

'He'll come around,' Kate had said to her when she came back up. 'Just give him time.'

But there was no more time as the taxi pulled in. Linda felt heartbroken and thrilled at the same time, with a little trepidation thrown into the mix for good measure. She hugged each of them in turn, including Peter, before hastily getting into the car to hide her tears from them. In the hour-long drive to the airport, she had plenty of time to reflect on her actions, nearly losing her nerve a couple of times, on the verge of asking the driver to take her back. But, with Kate's words ringing in her head, she knew couldn't back down now.

Glancing at her phone as they pulled up to the departure terminal, she was gutted to see that there was no message from

Scott. She'd felt sure he would have sent her something. Even a bon voyage would have done, but there was nothing.

Paying the driver and giving him a hefty tip as he helped take her bag out of the trunk, she took one last look around at Corfu. The island had been so important in changing her in so many ways; she would never forget it, and silently promised that she would come back one day before walking resolutely into the terminal.

As they watched the Mercedes carry Linda away, another, less glamorous car had turned into the drive and pulled up in front of them. It was the chef that they had booked for their final meal, arriving exactly on time, his car filled with produce and equipment ready to create a feast for them.

'We can shut that now,' said Pete, the departing taxi reminding him that the technician had messaged him earlier on to say the gate was working again. He hit the button on the console by the front door, causing the gates to judder to a close.

'Good evening, Spiro,' he called to the young man getting out of the car and went to shake the chef by the hand before helping him carry his supplies into the kitchen. As they walked, he explained to the chef that there would actually be six for dinner. Seeing the look of horror on the man's face, he felt the need to explain further 'you see, I'm joining the group because, well, because I have been invited, and Ms Delaney has asked another guest also.'

Thumping the box he was carrying onto the counter, the chef let out a stream of expletives in Greek, cursing the change of numbers and complaining that he wasn't Jesus, ready to feed the five thousand with so little food. Laughing at the typical artistic outburst, Peter said 'It will be fine, Spiro' and added in Greek that if needs be, he would accept very small portions in an effort to help spread the food around.

Slightly mollified by Peter's statement and his effort to speak in his language, Spiro gave a grim little smile as he tied on his apron and started unpacking the food. Peter was looking forward to the evening meal. With Pericles joining them and Manolis coming over much later, after he had finished working on the boat, it looked like being a fun night.

As she wouldn't see Manolis until later, Charlotte went to sit and chat with the boys in the kitchen. For once, she could enjoy the camaraderie rather than worrying what to say next or how she was looking. It was a wonderful feeling, being freed from all the self-imposed restraints of old. She was beginning to love just being herself and not giving two hoots what other people thought.

Down in his room, Scott was feeling desolate. The veneer of bravado that he had been so determined to keep in place had nearly cracked when Linda had come down to talk to him, leaving him incapable of speaking to her for fear he would break down and beg her not to go.

He had also received an email from the ever-vigilant Jean expressing her concerns over the River Oaks sale, the attorneys for the buyers seemed to be dragging their heels and she had a feeling that the couple may have had a change of heart, or found another property. It seemed to him that everything was falling apart around him and he didn't know what to do.

And now, the sounds of Linda's departure having filtered through to his room despite him trying to drown it out with his favourite Spotify playlist, he was prostrate on his bed, face down in the pillows, wrestling with his emotions. There was a tentative knock on his door, which he ignored, but Kate barged in anyway, refusing to pander to her son's tantrums any more now than she had when he was small.

'Scott Delaney, stop sulking in here and do something sensible' she said, automatically reaching down to pick up the clothes he'd discarded on the floor and folding them neatly on the chest of drawers.

'I'm not sulking,' came the muffled response from the pillows. 'Leave me be, Ma, I want to be by myself right now.'

She stood looking down at her son, who had been her whole world for so long and who was now evidently in so much pain as he lay, inert and hiding from the world. She knew he loved Linda; she was sure of that, but she also knew he felt excessively obligated to his father and, of course, to her, and that was mostly her fault.

She sat down next to him and placed her hand on his back, rubbing it gently the way she had when he needed soothing as a small boy.

'Scotty, I admire Linda. What she is doing right now is leaping into the unknown, which is scary whatever age you are. If you love her as much as I think you do, you should do the same and follow that girl as fast and as far as you can... For as long as you can.' she added, gazing into the middle distance as she considered her situation.

He shifted a fraction, turning his face towards her, and it broke her heart to see the tracks of his silent tears.

'Ma, you know I can't go running off at the drop of a hat. What about work? What about you?'

'Work will manage just fine without you and, as for your father, if he has anything to say on the matter, you can remind him that running off at the drop of a hat might be hereditary. He's in no position to lecture you on the matter.'

Scott turned a little more to look up at her, a glimmer of hope in his eyes.

'As for me,' she continued, 'I would never forgive myself if you lived a broken-hearted existence because you felt I couldn't cope on my own. This trip has shown me so many things, but the ultimate thing I am taking away with me is the fact that I know I can do things by myself. I have no idea what I am going to do next, but I am filled with excitement to leap, like Linda, into the unknown and see where it takes me. You should do the same, Scotty, grab the bull by the horns, get yourself to that damn airport and catch that girl!'

He sat up then, his face filled with a Pandora's Box of emotions, all his thoughts battling for resolution plainly writ across his face until, after the internal struggle, he was finally left with hope. As he broke into a smile, she knew he had reached the right decision and it filled her heart with joy to see his face light up again.

'Shit, you're right,' he said, leaping up and emptying things out of his bag onto the bed before throwing things randomly back in. 'I'm gonna have to take the car, Ma. Hope you don't mind?'

Kate laughed, noticing the velvet ring box forgotten in the pile on the bed 'I am sure I will manage. I told you, I am quite capable of dealing with things now. You go ahead and do what you need to do'

He stopped his frantic packing and went over and enveloped her in a bear hug, almost lifting her off the ground.

'I love you, Ma,'

'I love you too, Scotty,' she said, a lump forming in her throat. 'Now go git that girl!'

The others were startled when Scott came bounding up the stairs, taking them two at a time in his haste.

'Peter, I'm going to the airport,' he announced. 'I'll have to leave the car there... I'm not coming back,' he added happily.

Charlotte let out a whoop, pumping a fist in the air, and Peter smiled at him from his seat on the sofa next to Marc.

'Not a problem. Leave the key under the driver's mat. I'll organise to get it collected.'

Scott went running out the door, then hesitated and came back in.

'About bloody time, mate,' he said, looking at Marc.

'You knew?'

'I was born at night, but not last night. I've been waiting for you to come out since we were 12!'

Marc grinned sheepishly. 'Better late than never, I guess. Good luck, dude.'

There was a persistent hooting outside the gates. 'That'll be Pericles,' said Kate, grinning like a teenager and walking over to the console to press the button to open the gates.

Scott had run out and thrown his bag on the backseat of the car and jumped into the driver's seat, but when he turned the key in the ignition, nothing happened. He tried again; still nothing. He began to hit the steering wheel, cursing loudly. 'Stupid damn car!' he shouted, pointlessly turning the key and pressing the gas pedal again and again.

The horn outside the gate sounded again. The gates had failed to open beyond a few inches, grinding to a halt with a loud bang and sparks erupting out of the motor housed on the gatepost.

Scott looked desperately at his watch. The time seemed to be flying by and he was beginning to think that he would never make the flight and catch Linda before she disappeared. He had no idea what her connecting flights were, and he knew if he didn't find her now, it might take days to track her down. He couldn't bear the thought of her spending another minute thinking he didn't love her enough to travel to the ends of the world with her.

Peter had run-up to the gates with the override key and was trying frantically to open them manually, which was a painfully slow process. Scott leapt out of the car and ran up to the gates; he took one look at the small gap between them, threw his bag over and began to force his body through the slither of space that stood between him and happiness. With an expulsion of air that sounded like a balloon being let down at speed, he jimmied his way through them and almost fell onto Pericles, waiting on the other side.

'I have to get to the airport,' he panted at the older man. 'It's urgent. I have to catch the woman I love!'

Pericles's face broke into a huge smile. 'Eros strikes again!' he shouted gleefully and jumped back onto his bike, kicking it smoothly into action as Scott scooped up his bag and climbed on behind him.

'See you soon my love' Pericles called back to Kate with a wave through the partially open gates, and they shot up the track as fast as the potholes would allow.

The journey to the airport passed in a blur for Scott, some of it with his eyes closed if he was honest, his thoughts racing at what he was about to do. He knew his father was going to be furious and this impetuous decision could well mean the end of his career with the firm, but he abruptly realised he didn't care.

As the miles sped by, he felt the weight of years of unseen pressures shedding like a second skin, so by the time they reached the airport, he felt reborn. No longer Scott Delaney, the top salesman at Delaney Real Estate who did everything to please his parents, but Scott Delaney, a man so in love he would follow his girlfriend wherever she wanted to be and unconcerned by the monthly targets that had dominated his life for so long. It felt incredible.

Pericles deposited him at the domestic departures, slapped him on the back and said 'Kalo Taxidi, my friend,' and watched as the young man ran through the sliding doors so fast they barely had time to open. Scott skidded to a halt in the brightly lit airport, feverishly looking for signs of Linda. He glimpsed what he thought might be the back of her head just passing through the security control ahead of him. To his right was the desk for Aegean Air, so he ran over, waiting impatiently behind the queue until he could slap his credit card and passport on the desk.

'A ticket to Athens please,' he said, 'one way, no hold baggage, no extras, just a ticket as fast as you can.'

The young girl behind the counter smiled at this earnest young American 'You'll have to be quick, sir; they are starting to board.' She swiped his card and gazed at the screen, waiting for it to go through, and then frowned. 'I'm sorry sir, it doesn't seem to be working,' she said, looking at the card. 'Ah, I see. It's an Amex card, we have problems processing those. Do you have another?'

Scott rummaged frantically through his bag to unearth his emergency card; thank god he had that with him. He handed it over, hopping from foot to foot in agitation as he heard the final call for the flight to Athens, adrenaline coursing through him at this threat to his happiness.

She tapped away again at her computer until at last came the welcome sound of a boarding pass being printed. He snatched it out of her hand and sped through security, throwing his bag and belt into the container for it to be scanned before grabbing them from the other side and running over to the gate where the stewardess was making a move to close the door.

As he settled into his seat at the back of the plane, craning to try and see where Linda was, his phone beeped, announcing a message. At the stewardess's command, he strapped on his seatbelt and looked at the message from his father going on at length about how irresponsible he was letting this deal fall through and how much work he was going to have to do to make up for the loss of revenue. Scott stared at it for a moment before typing ***I quit*** and hitting the send button, switching off his phone with a grin and settling back into his seat to wait for the seatbelt sign to turn off so he could go and find Linda.

Later that night, as they sat around the candlelit table enjoying the freshly cooked meal that their chef had prepared for them, the group chatted happily, laughing at the week's turn of events as night fell like a star-studded cloak over the island. The warm air and starlit skies provided the perfect ambience for their final dinner on this glorious island, which had made such an enormous difference to all their lives.

'It's a good job Linda isn't here,' said Charlotte through mouthfuls of the amazing prawn Saganaki that accompanied the intricate salads and herbed rice. 'She would have pitched a hissy fit at all this seafood for sure!'

Kate nodded in agreement, wondering how on earth she could have been so blind to the fact that she had constantly, albeit subconsciously, ignored something so vital to the girl's well-being. She didn't need a psychiatrist to tell her that there must have been an element of jealousy involved; her need to look after her baby boy and her fear of losing him, her main purpose in life, had meant she treated the girl appallingly.

Pericles, who'd arrived back in time to join them for the main course, smiled at her knowingly across the table. She did not doubt that he understood what was running through her mind. He seemed so in tune with her thoughts and desires it was downright scary at times. She could hide nothing from him, it seemed, and she didn't want to. Secrets and deception had been the bane of her life with Danial, and there was no way she was going to endure that again from either side.

As the plates were cleared away by Spiros' helper, Kate raised her wineglass to make a toast. She smiled at them all, Peter and Marc so obviously enthralled in each other, Charlotte looking so happy even though she kept checking the time as she waited for Manolis and, last but not least, dear sweet Pericles. This man who'd swept her off her feet and shown her how to love and have fun again in just a few short days. She held his gaze for a beat.

'Here's to Linda and Scott, wherever they may end up. I hope their journey together is a happy one,' she announced. There was a murmur of 'here, here' from around the table and a resounding 'yammas!' from Pericles. Marc raised his glass again and said, 'and here's to Corfu, not only is it beautiful, it is truly life changing. I think we can all agree on that.' This was greeted with louder cries of assent and laughter from them all.

Charlotte squealed and jumped up as Manolis walked out onto the terrace, throwing herself on him and attaching her lips to his like a limpet. Pericles and Kate picked up the espresso they had requested rather than dessert, both being too full to contemplate the array of local ice creams no matter how amazing they were, and walked over to the wall of the terrace and looked out to the moonlit sea.

'Thank you again for taking Scotty to the airport,' she said. 'I don't know what he would have done without you.'

''It was no big thing,' he replied, turning to face her. 'But what about you? What are you going to do without me?'

Placing her cup on the wall next to his, she looked at him. 'I've been thinking about that. In fact, I've been thinking about little else and I just don't know. These last few days have been the happiest of my life and that is all because of you. I can't believe that tomorrow I am going to be on a plane, flying away from you,' she said mournfully, tears threatening to fall yet again as they had every time she contemplated life without this man.

Unable to bear seeing her so distressed, he took her in his strong arms and held her close 'Agapi mou, you have to do what is right for you,' he said softly. 'You have to do what makes you happy. We all do. Life is too short for anything else.'

ONE YEAR LATER

From: KateSalvanos@yahoo.gr

To: PeterWilliams@sublimeretreats.com

Subject: Corfu Vacation

Dear Peter,

It was so lovely to hear from you!

Of course, you and Marc are welcome to come and stay with Pericles and me next month, we have plenty of space in the villa and it will be perfect timing, Scott and Linda are due back at some point then, although they may decide to carry on travelling. They seem to be making up their journey as they go along; they have covered half the globe already, but it never seems enough, and good for them.

Charlotte is still here. She worked out the summer at the Surf School and she and Manolis are practically running it now. I have a feeling that she has found herself; she seems so very happy, much more carefree than the girl I used to know in Houston. We both are.

I have put my talents to good use and have been helping the animal charities here on the island. They were woefully disorganised, but I have knocked them into shape. We have regular events for fundraising and now there is a systematic programme of neutering and care in place, which is making a big difference to the stray population here. I am looking to start an educational program in the schools as well. Teaching the younger generation how to treat the world around them is a big part of my plans.

I am not surprised to hear you have been promoted to manager in the Denver head office of Sublime Retreats; you are perfect for that role and, should I decide to take a trip at any point, I will be calling you. Hard to imagine leaving this beautiful island though, and I would positively have to force Pericles.

As for the arrangements, I will be delighted to help! Let me know your flight details and I will send a taxi to meet you; I look forward to seeing you both again.

Regards,

Kate

Mrs Kate Salvanos

One month later, as they walked hand in hand down the sandy Kalamaki beach below Kate's new home, Marc couldn't believe how much his life had changed since he was last here.

He had found the courage to come out to his family, which had been rough going for quite a while, but they had, if not welcomed his new status, certainly come to accept it. Mostly because of his ma, if he was to be honest, who had always had a special place in her heart for her youngest son, and because of Petey. Aside from the fact he'd got his family a discount membership at Sublime Retreats, he was just plain likeable. His amazing people skills had, in the end, won over his Pa, and after that, the rest of his family had crumbled, knowing when they were beaten.

As the two men walked up a faded jetty that was looking a trifle perilous but still standing despite the constant beating from the tides, he thanked his lucky stars for Corfu and the magic it had brought to all of their lives last year.

When Peter dropped to his knee a few minutes later and Marc, with tears streaming unashamedly down his face, nodded emphatically, unable to speak in his joy, there was a loud series of whoops and hollering from the restaurant that had seemed closed behind them. Turning around in surprise, Marc wiped the tears from his face as realisation dawned and he recognised the people streaming over the beach to congratulate them. He tried and failed to glare at his Petey before going to meet the crowd of friends and family that were waiting to celebrate 'their moment' with them.

Milton Keynes UK
Ingram Content Group UK Ltd.
UKHW010653261023
431376UK00001B/38